"You're Delightfully Repressed," He Told Her.

The look in his eyes was all tenderness.

"It's safer that way around you," she mumbled.

He caught her arm as she started past him, and she felt the warmth of his body, like a drug.

"I want you to trust me," he said.

"Why?" she asked.

"Because if I take you with me to Central America, I'll want you with me all the time. Especially at night," he added.

She tingled from head to toe at the thought of lying in J.D.'s arms. It was something she'd contemplated for a long time, and hearing it from his lips almost made her gasp.

The flush in her cheeks told him everything....

SOLDIERS OF FORTUNE...prisoners of fate. Don't miss these thrilling tales of best buddies who become soldiers of love! The titles are: SOLDIER OF FORTUNE, THE TENDER STRANGER and ENAMORED!

Available from Diana Palmer

SOLDIER OF FORTUNE

Working for criminal lawyer J.D. Brettman was a full-time job for Gabby Darwin. J.D. was demanding and never gave Gabby a second thought—until the unforeseen happened and the two had to travel to Central America and track down terrorist kidnappers.

THE TENDER STRANGER

Dani St. Clair's Mexican vacation turned into a romantic adventure when she met—and married—a total stranger. Though her impetuous decision had been based on pure attraction to Eric van Meer, Dani knew if she was to be a true wife, she'd have to find out what would make this dangerous man tender.

ENAMORED

The past had finally caught up with Diego Laremos, in the form of Melissa Sterling. He'd given up hope of ever seeing his runaway bride again. But fate and a shockingly familiar-looking little boy were about to change Diego's future.

Diana Palmer

SOLDIER OF FORTUNE

Silhouette Books

Published by Silhouette Books
America's Publisher of Contemporary Romance

SILHOUETTE BOOKS

ISBN 0-373-48292-2

SOLDIER OF FORTUNE

Copyright © 1985 by Diana Palmer

This edition published by arrangement with Harlequin Enterprises B.V.

® and TM are trademarks of Harlequin Enterprises B.V., used under
license. Trademarks indicated with ® are registered in the United States
Patent and Trademark Office, the Canadian Trade Marks Office and in
other countries.

Printed in U.S.A.

For R.D.M.,
and Irene, my lovely mother-in-law

Chapter One

Gabby was worried about J.D. It wasn't anything she could put her finger on exactly. He still roared around the office, slamming things down on his desk when he couldn't find notes or reminders he'd scribbled on envelopes or old business cards. He glared at Gabby when she didn't bring his coffee on the stroke of nine o'clock. And there were the usual missing files, for which she was to blame of course, and the incessant phone calls that interrupted his concentration. There was still the heavy scowl on his broad face, and the angry glitter in his brown eyes. But that morning he'd been pacing around his office, smoking like a furnace. And that was unusual. Because J.D. had given up smoking years before, even before she had come to work for the law firm of Brettman and Dice.

She still couldn't figure out what had set him off. She'd put a long-distance call through to him earlier, one that sounded like it came from overseas. The caller had sounded suspiciously like Roberto, his sister Martina's husband, from Sicily. Soon afterward, there had been a flurry of outgoing calls. Now it was silent, except for the soft sounds the computer made as Gabby finished the last letter J.D. had dictated.

She propped her chin on her hands and stared at the door with curious green eyes. Her long, dark hair was piled high on her head, to keep it out of her way when she worked, and loose strands of it curled softly around her face, giving her an even more elfin look than usual. She was wearing a green dress that flattered her graceful curves. But J.D. wouldn't notice her if she walked through the office naked. He'd said when he hired her that he'd robbed the cradle. And he hadn't smiled when he said it. Although she was twenty-three now, he still made the most frustrating remarks about her extreme youth. She wondered wickedly what J.D. would say if she applied for Medicare in his name. Nobody knew how old he was. Probably somewhere around forty; those hard lines in his face hadn't come from nowhere.

He was one of the most famous criminal lawyers in Chicago. He made waves. He ground up hostile witnesses like so much sausage meat. But before his entry into the profession five years earlier, nothing was known about him. He'd worked as a laborer by day and attended law school by night. He'd worked his way up the ladder quickly and efficiently with the help of a devastating intelligence that seemed to feed on challenge.

He had no family except for a married sister in Palermo, Sicily, and no close friends. He allowed no one to really know him. Not his associate Richard Dice, not Gabby. He lived alone and mostly worked alone, except for the few times when he needed some information that only a woman could get, or when he had to have Gabby along as a cover. She'd gone with him to meet accused killers in warehouses at midnight and down to the waterfront in the wee hours of the morning to meet a ship carrying a potential witness.

It was an exciting life, and thank God her mother back in Lytle, Texas, didn't know exactly how exciting it was. Gabby had come to Chicago when she was twenty; she'd had to fight for days to get her mother to agree to the wild idea, to let her work for a distant cousin. The distant cousin had died quite suddenly and, simultaneously, J.D. had advertised for an executive secretary. When she applied, it had taken J.D. only five minutes to hire her. That had been two years earlier, and she'd never regretted the impulse that had led her to his office.

Just working for him was something of a feather in Gabby's cap. The other secretaries in the building were forever pumping her for information about her attractive and famous boss. But Gabby was as secretive as he was. It was why she'd lasted so long as his secretary. He trusted her as he trusted no one else.

She was a paralegal now, having taken night courses at a local college to earn the title. She did far more than just type letters and run off copies on the copier. The office had added a computer system. She ran that, and did legwork for her boss, and frequently traveled with him when the job warranted it.

While she was brooding, the door opened suddenly. J.D. came through it like a locomotive, so vibrant and superbly masculine that she imagined most men would step aside for him out of pure instinct. His partner Richard Dice was on his heels, raging as he followed.

"Will you be reasonable, J.D.!" the younger man argued, his lean hands waving wildly, his red hair almost standing on end around his thin face. "It's a job for the police! What can you do?"

J.D. didn't even look at him. He paused at Gabby's desk, an expression on his face that she'd never seen before. Involuntarily, she studied the broad face with its olive complexion and deep-set eyes. He had the thickest, blackest eyelashes she'd ever seen. His hair was just as thick and had deep waves in it, threaded with pure silver. It was the faint scars on his face that aged him, but she'd never quite had the bravado to ask where and how he'd gotten them. It must have been some kind of man who put them there. J.D. was built like a tank.

"Pack a bag," he told Gabby, in a tone too black to invite questions. "Be back here in an hour. Is your passport in order?"

She blinked. Even for J.D., this was fast shuffling. "Uh, yes...."

"Bring lightweight things, it'll be hot where we're going. Lots of jeans and loose shirts, a sweater, some boots, and a lot of socks." He continued nonstop. "Bring that third-class radio license you hold. Aren't you kin to someone at the State Department? That might come in handy."

Her mind was whirling. "J.D. what's going...?" she began.

"You can't do this," Dick was continuing doggedly, and J.D. was just ignoring him.

"Dick, you'll have to handle my case load until I get back," he pressed on in a voice that sounded like thunder rumbling. "Get Charlie Bass to help you if you run into any snags. I don't know exactly when we'll be back."

"J.D., will you listen?"

"I've got to pack a few things," J.D. said curtly. "Call the agency, Gabby, and get Dick a temporary secretary. And be back here in exactly one hour."

The door slammed behind him. Dick cursed roundly and rammed his hands into his pockets.

"What," Gabby asked, "is going on? Will somebody please tell me where I'm going with my passport? Do I have a choice?"

"Slow down and I'll tell you what little I know." Dick sighed angrily. He perched himself on her desk. "You know that J.D.'s sister is married to that Italian businessman who made a fortune in shipping and lives in Palermo, Sicily?"

She nodded.

"And you know that kidnapping is becoming a fast method of funding for revolutionary groups?" he continued.

She felt herself going pale. "They got his brother-in-law?"

"No. They got his sister when she went alone on a shopping trip to Rome."

She caught her breath. "Martina? But she's the only family he has!"

"I know that. They're asking for five million dollars, and Roberto can't scrape it up. He's frantic. They told him they'd kill her if he involved the authorities."

"And J.D. is going to Italy to save her?"

"However did you guess?" Dick grumbled. "In his usual calm, sensible way, he is moving headfirst into the china shop."

"To Italy? With me?" She stared at him. "Why am I going?"

"Ask him. I only work here."

She sighed irritably as she rose to her feet. "Someday I'm going to get a sensible job, you wait and see if I don't," she said, her eyes glittering with frustration. "I was going to eat lunch at McDonald's and leave early so I could take in that new science-fiction movie at the Grand. And instead I'm being bustled off to Italy...to do what, exactly?'' she added with a frown. ''Surely to goodness, he isn't going to interfere with the Italian authorities?''

''Martina is his sister,'' Dick reminded her. ''He never talks about it, but they had a rough upbringing from what I can gather, and they're especially close. J.D. would mow down an army to save her.''

''But he's a lawyer,'' she protested. ''What is he going to do?''

''Beats me, honey.'' Dick sighed.

''Here we go again,'' she muttered as she cleared her desk and got her purse out of the drawer. ''Last time he did this, we were off to Miami to meet a suspected mob informer in an abandoned warehouse at two o'clock in the morning. We actually got shot at!'' She shuddered. ''I didn't dare tell my Mama what was going on. Speaking of my Mama, what am I supposed to tell her?''

''Tell her you're going on a holiday with the boss.'' He grinned. ''She'll be thrilled.''

She glared at him. ''The boss doesn't take holidays. He takes chances.''

"You could quit," he suggested.

"Quit!" she exclaimed. "Who said anything about quitting? Can you see me working for a normal attorney? Typing boring briefs and deeds and divorce petitions all day? Bite your tongue!"

"Then may I suggest that you call James Bond," he said, "and ask if he has any of those exploding matches or nuclear warhead toothpicks he can spare."

She gave him a hard glare. "Do you speak any Spanish?"

"Well, no," he said, puzzled.

She rattled off a few explicit phrases in the lilting tongue her father's foreman had used with the ranch hands back during her childhood. Then, with a curtsy, she walked out the door.

Chapter Two

Gabby had seen J.D. in a lot of different moods, but none of them could hold a candle to the one he was in now. He sat beside her as stiff as a board on the jet, barely aware of the cup of black coffee he held precariously in one big hand.

Worst of all was the fact that she couldn't think of anything to say. J.D. wasn't the kind of man you offered sympathy to. But it was hard just to sit and watch him brood without talking at all. She'd rarely heard him speak of his sister Martina, but the tenderness with which he described her had said enough. If he loved any human being on earth, it was Martina.

"Boss..." she began uneasily.

He blinked, glancing toward her. "Well?"

She avoided that level gaze. "I just wanted to say I'm sorry." Her long, slender fingers fidgeted with the skirt of the white suit she was wearing. "I know how hard it must be for you. There's just not a lot that people can do in these kinds of situations."

A peculiar smile touched his hard features for a moment. He swallowed a sip of coffee. "Think not?" he asked dryly.

"You aren't serious about not contacting the authorities?" she persisted. "After all, they've got those special teams now, and they even rescued that one kidnap victim..."

He glanced down at her. The look stopped her in mid-sentence. "That was a political kidnapping. This isn't. As for those special teams, Darwin, they're not infallible. I can't take risks with Martina's life."

"No," she said. She stared at his hands. They were so gracefully masculine, the fingers long and tapered and as dark olive as his face, with flat nails and a sprinkling of hair, like that curling around the watch on his wrist. He had powerful hands.

"You aren't afraid, are you?" he asked.

She glanced up. "Well, sort of," she confessed. "I don't really know where we're going, do I?"

"You should be used to that by now," he reminded her dryly.

She laughed. "I suppose so. We've had some adventures in the past two years."

He pulled out a cheroot and lit it, staring at her narrowly over the flame. "Why aren't you married?" he asked suddenly.

The question startled her. She searched for the right words. "I'm not sure," she said. "I suppose I just haven't bothered to get involved with anyone. Until four years ago, I was living in a small town in Texas. Then I came up here to work for a cousin, he died, you needed a secretary..." She laughed softly. "With all due respect, Mr. Brettman, you're kind of a never-ending job, if you know what I mean. It just isn't a nine-to-five thing."

"About which," he observed, "you've never once complained."

"Who could complain?" she burst out. "I've been around the country and halfway across the world, I get to meet gangsters, I've been shot at . . . !"

He chuckled softly. "That's some job description."

"The other secretaries in the building are green, simply green, with envy," she replied smugly.

"You aren't a secretary. You're a paralegal. In fact," he added, puffing on his cheroot thoughtfully, "I've thought about sending you to law school. You've got a lot of potential."

"Not me," she said. "I could never get up in front of a courtroom full of people and grill witnesses like you do. Or manage such oration in a summing up."

"You could still practice law," he reminded her. "Corporate law, if you like. Or deal in estates and partnerships. Divorces. Land transfers. There are many areas of law that don't require oratory."

"I'm not sure enough that it's what I want to do with the rest of my life," she said.

He lifted his chin. "How old are you?"

"Twenty-three."

He shook his head, studying the chignon, the glasses she used for close reading and now had perched on top of her head, the stylish white linen suit she was wearing, the length of her slender legs. "You don't look it."

"In about twenty years could you repeat that?" she asked. "By then I'll probably appreciate it."

"What do you want to be?" he asked, persisting as he leaned back in the seat. His vested gray silk suit emphasized the sheer size of him. He was so close she could even feel the warmth of his body, and she found it oddly disturbing.

"Oh, I don't know," she murmured, glancing out the window at the clouds. "A secret agent, maybe. A daring industrial spy. A flagpole sitter." She looked over her shoulder at him. "Of course, those jobs would seem very dull after working for you,

Boss. And do I ever get to know where we're going?''

"To Italy, of course," he replied.

"Yes, sir, I know that. *Where* in Italy?"

"Aren't you curious, though?" he mused, lifting one shaggy eyebrow. "We're going to Rome. To rescue my sister."

"Yes, sir, of course we are," she said. It was better to agree with maniacs, she told herself. He'd finally snapped. It was even predictable, considering the way he'd been pushing himself.

"Humoring me, Miss Darwin?" he asked. He leaned deliberately past her to crush out his cheroot, and his face was so close that she could smell the spicy cologne he wore, feel the warm, smoky scent of his breath. As his fingers left the ashtray, he turned his head.

That look caused her the wildest shock she'd ever felt. It was like an earth tremor that worked its way from her eyes to the tips of her toes and made them want to curl up. She hadn't realized how vulnerable she was with him until her heart started racing and her breath strangled in her throat.

"I hesitated about taking you with me," he said quietly. "I'd rather have left you behind. But there was no one else I could trust, and this is a very delicate situation."

She tried to act normally. "You do realize that what you're thinking about could get her killed?"

"Yes," he said simply. "But not to act could get her killed quicker. You know what usually happens in these cases, don't you?"

"Yes, I do," she admitted. Her gaze moved down to his broad mouth with its lips that seemed sculpted from stone and back up again to his dark eyes. He looked different so close up.

"I'm doing what I think is best," he said. His fingers nudged a wisp of hair back into place at her neck, and she felt trembly all over from the touch. "We're not sure that the kidnappers still have Martina in Italy. Roberto thinks he knows one of them—the son of an acquaintance, who also happens to own land in Central America. I don't have to tell you what a hell of a mess this could turn into if they take Martina there, do I?"

She felt weak all over. "But how are they dealing with Roberto?"

"One of the group, and there is a group, is still in Italy, to arrange the handling of the money," he answered. He let his eyes fall to the jacket of her suit, and he studied it absently with disturbing concentration. "We may do some traveling before this is all over."

"But first we're going to Italy," she murmured dazedly.

"Yes. To meet some old friends of mine," he said, his chiseled mouth smiling faintly. "They owe me a favor from years past. I'm calling in the debt."

"We're taking a team?" she asked, eyebrows shooting up. It was getting more exciting by the minute.

"My, how your eyes light up when you speak of working with a team, Miss Darwin," he mused.

"It's so gung ho," she replied self-consciously. "Kind of like that program I watch on TV every week, about the group that goes around the world fighting evil?"

"*The Soldiers of Fortune?*" he asked.

"The very one." She grinned. "I never miss a single episode."

"In real life, Miss Darwin," he reminded her, "it's a brutal, dangerous occupation. And most mercenaries don't make it to any ripe old age. They either get killed or wind up in some foreign prison. Their lives are overromanticized."

She glowered at him. "And what would you know about it, Mr. Criminal Attorney?" she challenged.

"Oh, I have a friend who used to sell his services abroad," he replied as he sat back in his seat. "He could tell you some hair-raising stories about life on the run."

"You know a real ex-merc?" she asked, eyes widening. She sat straight up in her seat. "Would he talk to me?"

He shook his head. "Darwin." He sighed. "What am I going to do with you?"

"It's your fault. You corrupted me. I used to lead a dull life and never even knew it. Would he?"

"I suppose he would." His dark eyes wandered slowly over her. "You might not like what you found out."

"I'll take my chances, thanks. He, uh, wouldn't be one of the old friends you're meeting in Rome?" she asked.

"That would be telling. Fasten your seat belt, Darwin, we're approaching the airport now."

Her eyes lingered on his dark, unfathomable face as she complied with the curt order. "Mr. Brettman, why did you bring me along?" she asked softly.

"You're my cover, honey," he said, and smiled sideways at her. "We're lovers off on a holiday."

"The way I look?" she chided.

He reached over and took the pins out of her coiffure, loosening her hair. His fingers lifted the glasses from their perch atop her head, folded them, and stuffed them into his shirt pocket. He reached over again and flicked open the buttons of her blouse all the way down to the cleft between her high breasts.

"Mr. Brettman!" she burst out, pushing at his fingers.

"Stop blushing, call me Jacob, and don't start fighting me in public," he said gruffly.

"If you can remember all that, we'll do fine."

"Jacob?" she asked, her fingers abandoning their futile efforts to rebutton her buttons.

"Jacob. Or Dane, my middle name. Whichever you prefer, Gabby."

He made her name sound like bowers of pink roses in bud, like the softness of a spring rain on grass. She stared up at him.

"Jacob, then," she murmured.

He nodded, his dark eyes searching hers. "I'll take care of you, Gabby," he said. "I won't let you get in the line of fire."

"You meant it, didn't you?" she asked. "You're going to try to rescue Martina."

"Of course," he replied calmly. "She and I, we had a tough time as kids. Our father drowned in a bathtub, dead drunk, when we were toddlers. Mama scrubbed floors to keep us in school. As soon as we were old enough, we went to work, to help. But I was barely fifteen when Mama died of a heart attack. I've taken care of Martina ever since, just the way I promised I would. I can't let strangers try to help her. I have to."

"Forgive me," she said gently, "but you're an attorney, not a policeman. What can you do?"

"Wait and see," he told her. His eyes surveyed her quietly, approving her elfin beauty. "I'm not in my dotage yet."

"Yes, sir, I know that," she murmured.

"Jacob," he repeated.

She sighed, searching his dark eyes. "Jacob," she agreed.

That seemed to satisfy him. He glanced past her as the plane started down, and he smiled. "The Eternal City, Gabby," he murmured. "Rome."

She followed his gaze and felt her heart lift as the ancient city came into view below. Already, she was leaping ahead to the time when she could actually see the Colosseum and the Forum and the Pantheon. But as she remembered the reason for their being in Rome, her enthusiasm faded. Of course there wouldn't be time for sightseeing, she reasoned. J.D. was going to be too busy trying to get himself killed.

The drive into Rome was fascinating. They went in on the Viale Trastevere, through the old part of the city, across the wide Tiber on an ancient bridge. The seven hills of Rome were hardly noticeable because of centuries of erosion and new construction, but Gabby was too busy gaping at the ruins they passed to notice or care.

They went right by the Colosseum, and her eyes lingered on it as they proceeded to their hotel.

"We'll find a few minutes to see it," J.D. said quietly, as if he knew how much it meant to her.

Her gaze brushed his hard face and impulsively she touched her fingers to the back of his hand. "It really isn't that kind of a trip," she said softly.

He searched her worried face. His big hand turned, grasping hers warmly in its callused strength. "We'll have to pretend that it is, for a day or so at least," he said.

"What are we going to do?" she asked nervously.

He drew in a slow breath and leaned back against the seat, handsome and rugged-looking in his vested suit. It strained against massive muscles, and she tingled at the sight.

J.D. had always affected her powerfully in a purely physical way. It pleased her eyes to look at him.

"I'm working on that. But one thing we'll be doing in the hotel," he added slowly, "is sharing a suite. Will that frighten you?"

She shook her head. "I'm not afraid of anything when I'm with you, Jacob," she replied, finding that his given name was more comfortable to her tongue than she'd expected.

He cocked a heavy eyebrow. "That wasn't the kind of fear I meant, actually," he murmured. "Will you be afraid of me?"

"Why would I be?" she asked, puzzled.

He blew out a harsh breath and looked out the window. "I can't think of a single damned reason," he growled. "I hope Dutch got my message. He's supposed to call me later at the hotel."

"Dutch?" she queried softly.

"A man I know. He's my go-between with Roberto," he replied.

"Roberto and Martina don't live in Rome, do they?" she asked.

He shook his head. "In Palermo. So, for all appearances, we'll be a couple on holiday, and there won't be anything to connect us with the kidnapping."

"Will this man Dutch know if Martina is still in the country?" she asked.

"He'll know," he said with certainty.

He was obviously irritated with her, so she didn't press him with any more questions, contenting herself with staring at every building they passed.

Their hotel was disappointingly modern, but the old-world courtesy of the Italian desk clerk made up for it. He was attentive and outgoing, and Gabby liked him at once. J.D., however, seemed to have misgivings about him. He didn't share them with her, but he stared aggressively at the poor little man.

He had booked them a suite, with two bedrooms. Gabby hadn't expected anything else, but J.D.'s behavior was downright odd. He glared at the elegant sitting room, he glared at her, and he especially glared at the telephone. He paced and smoked, and Gabby felt as if she were going to fly apart, he made her so nervous. She went into her bedroom and unpacked, just to have something to do. The sudden sound of the phone ringing startled her, but she didn't go back into the sitting room; she waited for J.D. to call her. Meanwhile, she changed into jeans and a silky green top, leaving her hair loose and her reading glasses in her purse. She did look like a tourist on holiday. That ought to perk up J.D.

He called to her about five minutes later, and she walked into the room to find him staring blankly out the window. He'd taken off his jacket and vest and opened the top buttons of his shirt. His thick, wavy hair was mussed, and one big, tanned hand was still buried in it. A smoking cigarette was in the other hand, which was leaning on the windowsill.

"Jacob?" she murmured.

He turned. His dark eyes focused on her slender figure, so intent that they missed the shocked pleasure in her own gaze as she took in this sudden and unexpected glimpse of his body. Where the shirt was loose, she could see the olive tan of his chest under curls of dark hair, and rippling muscles that made her hands itch. Her whole body reacted to his sensuality, going rigid with excitement.

"Dutch," he said, nodding toward the phone to indicate who his caller had been. "Martina's out of the country."

She caught her breath. "Where?"

"Guatemala. On a *finca*—a farm—owned by a revolutionary group."

Her eyes searched his hard face. "Why would they take her there?"

"Terrorism is international, didn't you know? They probably have holdings all over the world, but Guatemala is in such a state of unrest it's a good place to hide a kidnap victim." He laughed bitterly. His jaw tautened. "They'll kill her if they don't get the money. They may do it anyway."

"What are you going to do?"

"I've already done it," he replied. "I've given Dutch a sum of money to buy some things I'll need. I've also had him contact my old comrades. They'll meet us at the Guatemalan *finca* of a friend of mine."

She cocked her head at him, uncomprehending. "When do we leave?"

"Tomorrow," he said. "As much as I'd like to jump on the next plane, we can't do it that way. I need time to plan. And there's no sense in signaling our every move. Dutch was going to speak to Roberto for me tonight. I'll need to know the status of his fund-raising before we leave."

"Will we fly into Guatemala?" she asked, feeling jittery.

"To Mexico," he said in answer. He smiled slowly. "As part of the holiday, of course," he added. "That will be broadcast to the right quarters."

"And now?" she asked. "What do I do?"

"We'll go see some of those ruins, if you like," he said. "It will help to pass the time."

Her eyes searched his. "I know you're worried, J.D. If you'd rather stay here..."

He moved closer to her, and the sudden proximity of his big body made her knees go weak. She lifted her face and found his dark eyes intent and unblinking.

"I don't think that's a good idea," he said quietly. He reached out and traced a slow path down her cheek to her throat, where her pulse went suddenly wild. "What would you like to see first?"

She found that her voice wobbled alarmingly. "How about the Forum?"

His dark eyes searched hers for a long moment. His fingers went to her mouth, touching it lightly, as if the feel of it fascinated him. His thumb dragged slowly, sensuously, over it, smearing her lipstick, arousing every nerve ending she had. She gasped, and her lips parted helplessly.

"The Forum?" he murmured.

She hardly heard him. Her eyes were held by his. Her body was reacting to the closeness of his in a new and frightening way. She could smell the musky cologne he wore and it made her head spin.

Her hands went to his chest in a small gesture of protest, but the feel of all that bare skin and matted hair made her jerk back.

He glanced down at her recoiling fingers with an odd expression. "It's only skin," he said quietly. "Are you afraid to touch me?"

"I've never touched anybody that way," she blurted out.

He tipped her face up to his and studied it with an odd smile. "Haven't you? Why?"

What an interesting question, she thought. What a pity she didn't have an answer.

"Don't tell me you haven't had the opportunity, Gabby," he said softly. "I wouldn't believe it."

"Mama said that it wasn't wise to do things like that to men," she told him doggedly, her chin thrust out. "She said they were hard enough to manage even when it didn't go beyond kissing."

"So there," he added for her with a faint smile. "She was right. Men get excited easily when they want a woman."

She felt the blush go up into her hairline, setting fire to her face. And he laughed, the horrible man!

She pulled away from him with a hard glare. "That was unkind," she grumbled.

"And you're delightfully repressed," he told her, but the look in his eyes was all tenderness. "You'd be pure sweet hell to initiate, Gabby."

"I don't want to be initiated," she said primly. "I want to see the Forum."

"All right, coward, hide your head in the sand," he taunted, holding the door open for her.

"It's safer that way, around you," she mumbled.

He caught her arm as she started past him, and she felt the warmth of his body like a drug. "I'll never hurt you," he said unexpectedly, drawing her stunned gaze to his face. It was hard and solemn. Almost grim. "You trust me in every other way. I want you to trust me physically as well."

"Why?" she asked.

"Because if I take you with me to Central America, I'll want you with me all the time. Especially at night," he added. "The men we'll be working with aren't particularly gentle. For all intents and purposes, you'll be my possession."

"To protect me from them?" she asked.

He nodded. "That means, in case you haven't worked it out, that you'll be sleeping in my bed."

She tingled from head to toe at the thought of lying in J.D.'s arms. It was something she'd contemplated in her own mind for a long time, and hearing it from his lips almost made her gasp. As it was, her flush told him everything anyway.

"In my bed," he repeated, searching her eyes. "In my arms. And I won't touch you in any way that I shouldn't. Even when we're back home and Martina is safe, and you're at your computer again, there won't be anything you'd be ashamed to tell your mother. All right?"

She couldn't find the words to express what she was feeling. J.D. felt protective of her. It was something she'd never expected. And uncharacteristically, she was disappointed. Did it mean that he didn't want her?

"All right, Jacob," she whispered softly.

His nostrils flared and his eyes flashed down at her. The hand holding her arm tightened until it hurt. "We'd better get out of here," he said gruffly. He let her go, turning away as if it took some effort, and opened the door.

Rome was the most exciting place Gabby had ever been. All of it seemed to be interspersed with history and crumbling ruins and romance. J.D. told her that the Colosseum, the Forum, the Ninfeo di Nerone—Nero's Sanctuary of the Nymphs—and the ruins of Nero's House of Gold residence were all near the Caelian, Capitolene, and Palatine hills. They decided to concentrate on that area of the city.

There was so much to see that Gabby's mind seemed to overload. They wandered around the ruins of the Forum first, and she just stared and stared like the eternal tourist.

"Just imagine," she whispered, as if afraid the ghosts might hear and take offense, "all those centuries ago Romans walked here just as we're walking today, with the same dreams and hopes and fears we feel. I wonder if they ever thought about how the world would be in the future?"

"I'm sure they did." J.D. stuck his hands in his pockets, and the wind ran like loving fingers through his crisp, dark hair. With his head thrown back like that, his profile in relief, he could have been one of the early Romans himself.

"Have you ever read *The Annals of Imperial Rome* by Tacitus?" she asked.

His head jerked around. "Yes. Have you?"

She grinned. "I was always a nut about Roman history. And Greek history. I loved Herodotus, even though he's been bad-mouthed a lot for some of his revelations."

"He was repeating what he'd heard or was told," he said. "But it's fascinating reading, nevertheless." He smiled amusedly. "Well, well, a historian. And I never suspected. I thought your knowledge of other countries was limited to those sweet little romance novels you read."

She glared at him. "I learn a lot about the world from those books," she said, defending herself. "And about other things too."

He cocked a dark eyebrow. "What other things?"

She looked away. "Never mind."

"We can go and see the catacombs later, if you like. They're south of here."

"Where the early Christians were buried?" She shuddered. "Oh, no, I don't think so. It's kind of an invasion of privacy. I'm sure I wouldn't want someone walking through my grave."

"I suppose it depends on your point of view," he conceded. "Well, we'll drive up to the Colosseum then."

"What was the other thing you mentioned, the Ninfeo di Nerone?"

He looked down at her with dark, indulgent eyes. "The Sanctuary of the Nymphs. You'd have fit right in, with your long, dark hair and mysterious eyes."

"I wouldn't have liked the debauchery," she said with certainty, her green eyes flashing. "The morals in Rome in Nero's time were decadent. I read that he had his wife Octavia killed, in a horrible way, after some prodding by his mistress."

"That was in Tacitus," he recalled. "A lot of terrible things happened here in the early days. But if you think about it, honey, terrible things are still happening. Like Martina's kidnapping."

"The world hasn't really changed very much, has it?" she asked sadly, watching the disturbance in his features at the thought of Martina and what she might be going through. She reached out and touched his arm gently. "They won't hurt her, Jacob," she said quietly. "Not until they get the money. Will they?"

"I don't know." He caught her arms and jerked her against his hard body, holding her there and staring intently into her eyes. "Frightened?" he asked on a husky note.

"No," she lied.

His dark eyes held hers. "We're supposed to be lovers on a holiday," he reminded her. "Just in case anyone is watching us..."

His head started to bend, and she caught her breath. Her eyes dropped to his chiseled mouth and she suddenly became breathless.

"Haven't you ever wondered?" he asked tautly, hesitating when he saw the shock on her young face.

Her eyes fluttered up to his fierce ones and back down again. "How it would be to...to kiss you?" she whispered.

"Yes."

Her lips parted on a rush of breath. She felt her breasts pressed softly against his shirtfront and was aware of the hardness of warm muscles against their hardening tips.

She felt trembly all over just at the touch of his body.

His hands slid up her arms, over her shoulders, and up her throat to cup her face and look at it with searching eyes.

"For the record," he murmured quietly, "is it a distasteful thought?"

That did shock her. She couldn't imagine any woman finding him distasteful.

"It's not that at all," she said. Her fingers flattened against his shirtfront, feeling the warm strength of his body. "I'm afraid that you'll be disappointed."

His eyebrows shot up. "Why?"

She moved restlessly. "I haven't kissed a lot of people. Well, you keep me too busy," she added defensively when his eyes twinkled.

"So your education has been neglected?" He laughed softly. "I'll teach you how to kiss, Gabby. It isn't hard at all. Just close your eyes and I'll do the rest."

She did, and the first contact with that hard, persuasive mouth made her breath catch. He lifted his head, studying her.

"What was that wild little gasp about?" he asked gently.

Her wide eyes searched his. "You're my boss...."

That seemed to anger him. "For today, I'm a man." His thumbs under her chin coaxed her face up still farther. His head bent, his mouth hovering just above hers. "Relax, will you?" he whispered. "I can hear your bones straining."

She laughed nervously. "I'm trying. You make me feel...stiff. I'm sorry, I'm kind of new at this."

"Stiff how?" He pounced on that, his expression giving nothing away, his eyes narrow and unblinking.

Her lips parted. Her fingers contracted on his shirtfront, her nails biting unconsciously into his chest, and he stiffened. "Now you're doing it too," she whispered.

His face relaxed, and there was a wild kind of relief in his dark eyes. He brushed his mouth over her forehead, her closed eyes. His hands slid behind her head and into the thick hair at her nape, cradling it.

"Gabby," he murmured as he tasted the softness of her cheeks, her forehead, "that stiffness . . . have you felt it before with anyone?"

It was a casual-sounding question, nothing to alarm her. "No," she murmured. She liked the soft, slow kisses he was pressing against her face. She felt like a child being loved.

"Would you like me to make it worse?"

She opened her dazed eyes to ask what he meant, and his open mouth crushed down on her lips. She gasped softly, letting her eyes close again. His mouth felt odd; it was warm and smoky tasting and very, very expert. Her fingers clung to the fabric of his shirt, twisting it into wrinkles. She stood quite still, her body tense with hunger, feeling the slow persuasion of his mouth grow rougher.

He lifted his mouth away from hers, his face so close that she couldn't see anything but his lips. "Who taught you that it was impolite to open your mouth when a man kissed it?" he whispered softly.

Her eyes went dazedly up to his dark ones. "Is it?" she whispered back, her voice sounding high-pitched and shaky.

"No," he breathed. His thumb gently tugged on her lower lip, coaxing her mouth open. "I want to taste you, Gabby. I want to touch you . . . inside . . ."

She started to tremble at the sensuality of the words and of his touch. His mouth eased hers open and slowly increased its hungry pressure. She felt the tiny bristle of a half day's growth of beard around his mouth and felt the hardness of his tongue slowly, delicately, penetrating her lips.

A tiny moan trembled in her throat.

"Don't be afraid," he whispered, his own voice oddly strained. "It won't hurt."

She did moan then, as the implied intimacy and the penetration all washed over her at once, and she drowned in the sensation of being possessed by him. He tasted of smoke and coffee, and her nails dug into his shoulders. She pressed her body into the hard curve of his and heard him groan.

"No," he said suddenly, pushing her away. He turned, walked off and lit a cigarette.

Gabby clutched her purse to her and stood staring helplessly after him, trembling all over. She'd never dreamed that it would feel like that!

Around them, a group of tourists was just entering the end of the Forum, which they'd had momentarily to themselves. Gabby got a glimpse of colorful clothing and heard murmuring voices as J.D. smoked his cigarette for several long moments before he turned and rejoined her.

"I shouldn't have done that," he said quietly. "I'm sorry."

She was struggling for composure, and it was hard won. "It's all right," she said. "I know you're worried about Martina..."

"Was I looking for comfort, Gabby?" He laughed mirthlessly. His dark eyes swept up and down her slender body.

"I'd rather it was that," she murmured, "than you needing a woman and having me get in the way."

"It wasn't that impersonal, I'm afraid," he said, falling into step beside her. He towered over her. "Gabby, I'll tell you something. I've done it in every conceivable way, with a hell of a lot of women. But up until now, I've never wanted a virgin."

She stopped and looked up at him, puzzled.

He glanced down at her. "That's right," he said. "I want you."

Her face flushed.

"You'll have to remind me at odd intervals that you're a virgin," he continued, smiling faintly. "Because I'm not really out of the habit of taking what I want."

He was angry and frustrated and probably trying to warn her off, she thought. But she wasn't afraid of him. "If you seduce me," she told him, "I'll get pregnant and haunt you."

He stared at her as if he didn't believe his ears. And then he threw back his dark head and laughed like a boy, his white teeth flashing in his dark face.

"Then I'll have to be sure I don't seduce you, won't I?" he teased.

She smiled up at him, feeling oddly secure. "Please."

He drew in a long breath as they walked, sighed and took another drag from his cigarette. "I thought this was all going to be straightforward and simple," he murmured. "Maybe I'd better put you on a plane back to Chicago, little one."

"Cold feet?" she muttered.

"Not me, lady. But you might wish you'd stayed home. I don't know where my mind was when I dragged you over here."

"You said you trusted me."

"I do. Totally. That's why I wanted you with me. The way things are turning out, I'm going to need you more than ever. When we get to my friend's *finca,*" he said quietly, "someone has to stay behind to handle communications. We'll have powerful walkie-talkies and we'll need updated information. The *finca* we'll be staying at is only miles from the one where Martina is being held."

She felt uneasy as she studied his hard face. "You're not going in there alone?"

"No—with those old friends I was telling you about."

"Couldn't you stay behind at your friend's finca?"

"Worried about me?" He laughed. "Gabby, I've dodged a lot of bullets in my time. I was in the Special Forces."

"Yes, you told me," she grumbled. "But that was a long time ago. You're a lawyer now, you sit behind a desk..."

"Not all the time," he said, correcting her. His eyes studied her quietly. "There are a lot of things you don't know about me. About my private life."

"You could get yourself killed."

"A car could hit me while I'm standing here," he countered.

She glared at him. "I'd be without work. One of the unemployed. Everything I'd do for the rest of my life would be horribly boring."

"I'd miss you too, I guess," he agreed, laughing. "Don't worry about me, Gabby. I can take it as it comes."

"Do I even get to meet this man you call Dutch?"

He shook his head. "You'll meet enough odd characters in Central America. And Dutch hates women."

"You aren't Mr. Playboy yourself," she muttered.

"Aren't you glad?" he asked, turning to look at her. "Would you like a man who had a different woman every night?"

The question shocked her. She struggled for an answer, but he'd already opened the door of the rental car and was helping her in.

The rest of the day went by in a haze. She went back to the hotel with him, her eyes full of ruins and Romans and maddening traffic. She had a bouquet of flowers that J.D. had bought from an old woman near the Fountain of Trevi. She couldn't wait to get into her room and press one of the flowers, to keep forever. She buried her nose in them lovingly.

Across the room, J.D. was speaking fluent Italian with someone on the phone. He hung up and turned back to her.

"I have to go out for a little while," he said. "Lock the door and let no one in, not even room service, until I get back. Okay?"

She studied him quietly. "You won't go getting into trouble while I'm not around to rescue you, will you?" she said, teasing him.

He shook his head. "Not a chance. Watch yourself."

"You too. Oh, Jacob!"

He turned with his hand on the door-knob. "What?"

"Thank you for the flowers."

"They suit you." He studied her face and smiled. "You look like one of them. *Ciao*, Gabby."

And he was gone. She stared at the door for a long time before she went to put her flowers in some water.

Chapter Three

J.D. didn't come back until late that afternoon, and he was strangely taciturn. He shared a silent supper with Gabby and then went out again, telling her tersely to get some sleep. She knew he'd found out something, but whatever it was, he wasn't sharing it. Apparently his trust in her had limits. And that was disappointing. She climbed into bed and slept soundly and without interruption. Part of her had hoped for a nightmare or an earthquake that would bring him running into her room. All her wild fantasies ended

with him running into her room and catching her up in his hard arms. She sighed. This
was certainly not the trip she'd envisioned.
It was turning into a wild tangle of new
emotions. A week before, she couldn't have
imagined that he would tell her he wanted
her.

They flew to Mexico the following morning. Several hours into the flight Gabby shot
a worried glance at J.D. He'd hardly moved
in his seat since takeoff, and she'd busied
herself looking at clouds and reading the
emergency instructions and even the label on
her jacket out of desperation.

He seemed to sense her searching gaze and
turned his head to look down at her.
"What's wrong?" he asked softly.

She made an odd little gesture. "I don't
know," she said inadequately.

His eyebrows lifted. "I'll take care of
you."

"I know that." She let her eyes fall to the
vest of his gray suit. "Will we stay in Mexico City?"

"Probably not. We're supposed to be met
at the airport." He reached over and took

her slender hand in his big one. The contact was warm and wildly disturbing, especially when she felt his thumb moving slowly, sensuously, against her moist palm. "Nervous?" he taunted.

"Oh, no. I always go running off into the dark unafraid," she replied with a grimace. She glanced up. "I come from a long line of idiots."

He smiled at her. It was a shock to realize that he'd smiled more at her in these two days than he had in two months back at the office. Her eyes searched the deep brown of his, and the airplane seemed to disappear. He returned the look, his smile fading. His nostrils flared and the hand holding hers began to move slowly, his fingers probing, easing between hers. It was so sensuous she felt herself tremble. His hand was pressed against hers, palm to palm, fingers tightly interlocked, and when it contracted it was almost an act of possession.

Her lips parted in a soft gasp, and his eyes narrowed.

"Bodies do that," he whispered under his breath, watching her reactions intently. "Just as slowly, just as easily."

"Don't," she protested brokenly, averting her face.

"Gabby," he chided gently, "don't be a child."

She ground her teeth together and struggled for composure. It wasn't easy, because he wouldn't let go of her hand despite her token protest.

"You're out of my league, Mr. Brettman," she said unsteadily, "as I'm sure you know. Don't... don't amuse yourself with me, please."

"I'm not." He sighed and turned sideways so that his head rested against the back of the seat. Then he coaxed her face around to his. "You've never known the kind of men you'll meet when we get where we're going. I thought," he continued, smiling at her stunned look, "that it might be easier for you if we got in a little practice along the way."

"What do you mean? What will we have to do...?" she began nervously.

"I mean, as I told you in Rome, that we'll have to be inseparable for the most part. We have to look as if we can't keep our hands off each other."

She stopped breathing, she knew she did. Her eyes wandered quietly over his face. "Is that why, at the Forum . . . ?"

He hesitated for an instant. "Yes," he said deliberately. "You were far too jumpy with me to be taken for my lover. It has to look convincing to do us any good."

"I see," she said, fighting to keep her disappointment from showing.

He studied her eyes, her cheeks, and then her mouth. "You have the softest lips, Gabby," he murmured absently. "So full and tempting; and I like the taste of them all too much . . ." He caught himself and lifted his eyes. "You'd better remind me at intervals that you're off-limits."

She was so aware of him that she tingled, and the thought that he might kiss her again made her go hot all over. She smiled strangely and looked away.

"What was that about, that tiny little smile?" he asked curiously.

"I never used to think of you that way," she confessed without thinking.

"How? As a lover?" he probed.

She lowered her eyes quickly. "Yes," she said shyly.

She felt his long fingers brush her cheek and then her neck, where the pulse was beating wildly.

"Oddly enough, I've hardly thought of you any other way," he said in a deep, gruff whisper.

Her lips opened as she drew a sharp breath, and she looked straight into his eyes. "J.D. . . .?" she whispered uncertainly.

His thumb brushed across her mouth, a tiny whisper of sensation that made her ache in the oddest places. His own breath wasn't quite steady, and he frowned, as if what was happening wasn't something he'd counted on or expected.

His eyes dropped to her parted lips and she heard him catch his breath. In a burst of nervousness, her tongue probed moistly at her dry upper lip and he made a rough sound in his throat. "Gabby, don't do that," he ground out. His thumb pressed hard against her mouth, and his head bent. "Let me..."

In a starburst of sensation, she felt the first tentative brush of his hard lips against her own.

And just as it began, it was suddenly over. The loudspeaker blared out a warning for passengers to fasten their seat belts, and the delicate spell was broken.

J.D. lifted his head reluctantly, his eyes almost black with frustration, his face pale. "The next time," he whispered gruffly, "I'll kiss the breath out of you, the way I wanted to at the Forum."

She couldn't answer him. She was swimming in deep waters, hungry for him in an unexpectedly desperate way. Her hands fumbled with her seat belt and she couldn't look at him. What was happening to them? she wondered, shaken. Just the morning before, they'd been employer and employee. And in a flash, they were something else, something frightening.

His hand caught hers, enfolding it. "Don't, please, be frightened of me," he said under his breath. "I won't hurt you. Not in any way, for any reason."

She glanced at him. "I'm all right," she said. "I'm just . . . just . . ."

"Stunned?" he asked wryly. "Join the crowd. It shocked me too."

Her eyes locked on their clasped hands. "But I thought you kissed me to—how did you put it—make it look better for the men?"

"I did. And to satisfy my own curiosity about you. And yours about me." He tilted her face up to his. "Now we know, don't we?"

"I think I'd be better off not knowing," she muttered.

"Really? At least now you've learned how to kiss."

"You have the diplomacy of a tank!" she shot at him.

He smiled, his teeth white against that olive tan. "You're spunky, Gabby. I'm glad. You're going to need spunk."

His words brought back the reason for their trip, and she frowned. The plane started to descend and she clung to J.D.'s strong fingers, wondering if in a few weeks this would all be nothing more than a memory. He'd said they'd have to seem involved; was this just a practice session? The frown deepened. She realized quite suddenly that she didn't want it to be. She wanted J.D. to kiss the breath out of her, as he'd threatened, and mean it.

They landed in Mexico City, and Gabby's eyes widened as they walked into the terminal. She smiled, dreams of Aztecs and ancient ruins going through her mind—until she remembered poor Martina, and the fact that they weren't here to look at tourist attractions.

She looked at J.D., standing tall and quiet at her side with a smoking cigarette in his hand. He stared slowly around the terminal while Gabby shifted restlessly beside him, their two small carry-on cases beside her.

After what seemed like a long time, J.D. began to smile as a tall, devastatingly attractive man strode toward them. He was wearing a beige suit and leather boots, and he looked debonair and a little dangerous—like J.D.

"Laremos." J.D. grinned as they shook hands.

"Did you think I'd forgotten you?" the other man asked in softly accented English. "You look well, Archer."

Gabby's eyebrows lifted curiously.

"Archer," the man explained, "is the name to which he answered many years ago, during our... acquaintance. You are Gabby Darwin, no?"

"Yes." She nodded. "And you are Señor Laremos?"

"Diego Laremos, *a sus ordenes,*" he said formally, bowing. He grinned. "A dish, Archer."

"Yes, I think so myself," J.D. said casually, smiling at her as he drew her unresisting body close to his side. "Did Dutch phone you?"

The smile faded and Laremos was at once something else, something out of Gabby's experience. "*Sí.* Drago and Semson and Apollo are here now."

"No sweat. How about my equipment?"

"Apollo got it from Dutch," Laremos said, his voice low and intent. "An Uzi and a new AK-47."

J.D. nodded while Gabby tried to decide what in the world they were talking about. "We'll need some RPGs."

"We have two," Laremos said. "And eight blocks of C-4, rockets for the RPGs, assorted paraphernalia, jungle gear, and plenty of ammo. The border is a massing point for the guerrillas these days—you can get anything if you have the money and the contacts."

J.D. smiled faintly. "Dutch said First Shirt has both. You made a smart move when you put him in charge of your ranch security."

"*Sí,*" Laremos agreed. "It is why I survive and many of my neighbors have not. The *finca* above mine was burned to the ground a month ago, and its owner..." He glanced at Gabby. "Forgive me, *señorita.* Such talk is not for the ears of women."

"I don't even understand it," she said, studying both men. "What is an RP..."

whatever it was? And what do you mean, rockets?''

"I'll tell you all about it later," J.D. promised. ''Got the plane?'' he asked Laremos.

The other man nodded. ''We will have to go through customs. I assume you have nothing on you that it would be embarrassing to declare when we land; otherwise you would not have made it through Mexican customs.''

J.D. chuckled. ''Even with you along, I doubt they'd look the other way if I boarded with the Uzi slung around my neck and clips of ammunition hanging out of my pockets.''

Laremos laughed too. ''Doubtless they would not. Come. We are gassed up and ready to go.''

"Uzi?'' Gabby queried as they followed him.

J.D. pulled her against him briefly. ''An Uzi is an Israeli-made weapon. It's classified as a semiautomatic.''

"Did you use one in the Special Forces?''

He laughed softly. ''No.''

"Then how do you...and why...and what...?"

He bent suddenly and pressed a hard, warm kiss on her startled mouth. "Shut up, Gabby, before you get us into trouble."

As if she could talk at all, after that. Her lips felt as though they'd been branded. If only they'd been alone, and it could have been longer...

Laremos had a twin-engine plane and a pilot to fly it. He settled into one of the comfortable seats in front of Gabby and J.D. and another man, small and young, brought them cups of coffee as the plane headed toward Guatemala City.

"I have told the appropriate people that you and your friend here are visiting me," Laremos said to J.D. and laughed. "It will put you under immediate suspicion I fear, because my past is no secret. But it will spare you the illegality of having to smuggle yourself across the border. I have friends high in government who will help. Oddly enough, the terrorists who have your sister attempted to kidnap me only weeks ago. First Shirt was nearby and armed."

"First Shirt doesn't miss," J.D. recalled.

"Neither did you, my friend, in the old days." Laremos studied the older man unsmilingly.

"How many men are there in the terrorist group?" J.D. asked. "Hard core, Laremos, not the hangers-on who'll cut and run at the first volley."

"About twelve," came the reply. "Maybe twenty more who will, as you say, cut and run. But the twelve are veteran fighters. Very tough, with political ties in a neighboring country. They are just part of an international network, with members in Italy who saw a chance to make some fast money to finance their cause. Your brother-in-law is an important man, and a wealthy one. And the decision to bring your sister here was most certainly devised by one of those twelve. They took over the *finca* only a month ago. I have little doubt that the kidnapping has been planned for some time." He shrugged. "Also, it is known that the Italian authorities have been successful in dealing with this sort of kidnapping. There is less risk here, so they smuggled her out of Italy."

"Roberto is trying to borrow enough to bargain with," J.D. said. "He's determined not to go to the authorities."

"He does not know about you, does he?" Laremos asked quietly.

J.D. shook his head. "I covered my tracks very well."

"You miss it, the old life?"

J.D. sighed. "At times. Not often anymore." He glanced at Gabby absently. "I have other interests now. I was getting too old for it. Too tired."

"For the same reasons, I became an honest man." Laremos laughed. "It is by far the better way." He stretched lazily. "But sometimes I think back and wonder how it would have been. We made good *amigos,* Archer."

"A good team," J.D. agreed. "I hope we still do."

"Have no fear, *amigo.* It is like swimming—one never forgets. And you, do you keep in condition?"

"Constantly. I can't get out of the habit," J.D. said. "Just as well that I have. Cutting through that jungle won't be any easy march. I've been keeping up with the situation down here, politically and militarily."

"What about this lovely one?" Laremos asked, frowning as he studied Gabby. "Is she a medic?"

"She'll handle communications," J.D. said shortly. "I want her at the ranch with you so that there's no chance she might get in the line of fire."

"I see." Laremos's dark eyes narrowed and he laughed. "Trust still comes hard to you, eh? You will never forget that one time that I let my mind wander..."

"No hard feelings," J.D. said quietly. "But Gabby runs the set."

Laremos nodded. "I understand. And I take no offense. My conscience still nags me about that lapse."

"Will somebody tell me, please, what's going on?" Gabby asked when she could stand it no longer.

"I've gotten together a group to get Martina out," J.D. said patiently. "That's all you need to know."

"The mercs! They're already here?"

"Yes," he murmured, watching her with a tiny smile on his face.

"Ah, I think the line of work of our *amigos* fascinates this one." Laremos grinned handsomely.

"Can I actually talk to them?" Gabby said, persisting, all eyes and curiosity. "Oh, J.D., imagine belonging to a group like that, going all over the world to fight for freedom."

"A lot of them do it for less noble reasons, Gabby," he said, searching her face with an odd intensity. "And you may be disappointed if you're expecting a band of Hollywood movie stars. There's nothing glamorous about killing people."

"Killing . . . people?"

"What in God's name did you think they did, turn water hoses on the enemy?" he asked incredulously. "Gabby, in war men kill each other. In ways you wouldn't like to know about."

"Well, yes, I realize that." She frowned. "But it's a very dangerous way to live, it's..." She stopped and searched for words. "Before I came to work for you I lived a quiet, kind of dull life, J.D.," she said, trying to explain. "Sometimes I thought that I'd probably never do anything more exciting than washing clothes at the Laundromat. Those men...they've faced death. They've learned the limits of their courage, they've tested themselves until the secrets are all gone." She looked up. "I don't suppose it makes sense, but I think I envy them in a way. They've taken all the veneer off civilization and come away with the reality of what they are. In a terrible way, they've seen the face of life without the mask. I never will. I don't think I really want to. But I'm curious about people who have."

He brushed the hair back from her face with a gentle hand. "When you see First Shirt, you won't have to ask questions. You'll be able to read the answers in his face. Won't she, Laremos?"

"But indeed." He chuckled.

"Is he a friend of yours?" she asked J.D.

He nodded. "One of the best I ever had."

"When you were in the Special Forces?" she asked.

He turned away. "Of course." He glanced at Laremos, and they exchanged a level gaze that Gabby didn't understand.

"You didn't want mines, did you?" Laremos asked suddenly.

"No. We could have carried in a few Claymores, but they're too much extra weight. The RPGs will be enough, and Drago can jury-rig a mine if he has to. I want to get in and get out fast."

"The rainy season hasn't started, at least," Laremos said. "That will be a bonus."

"Yes, it will. Have you still got my crossbow?"

"Above the mantel in my study." Laremos smiled. "It is a conversation piece."

"To hell with that, does it still work?"

"Yes."

"A crossbow?" Gabby laughed. "Is it an antique?"

J.D. shook his head. "Not quite."

"Is it easier to shoot than a bow and arrow?" she asked, pursuing the subject.

He looked uncomfortable. "It's just a memento," he said. "Gabby, did you pack some jeans and comfortable shoes?"

"Yes, as you saw in Italy." She sighed, beginning to feel uneasy. "How long will we be here?"

"Probably no more than three days, if things go well," he replied. "We need a little time to scout the area and make a plan."

"The hospitality of my *finca* is at your disposal," Laremos said. "Perhaps we might even make time to show Gabby some of the Maya ruins."

Her eyes lit up. "Really?"

"Don't mention archaeological ruins around her, please," J.D. muttered. "She goes crazy."

"Well, I like old things," she retorted. "Why else would I work for you?"

J.D. looked shocked. "Me? Old?"

She studied his face. It wasn't heavily lined, but there was a lot of silver at his temples mingling with his black hair. She frowned. She'd always assumed he was pushing forty, but now she wondered.

"How old are you, J.D.?" she asked.

"Thirty-six."

She gasped.

"Not what you expected?" he asked softly.

"You . . . seem older."

He nodded. "I imagine so. I've got thirteen years on you."

"You needn't sound so smug," she told him. "When I'm fifty, you'll hate those extra thirteen years."

"Think so?" he murmured, smiling.

She glanced away from that predatory look. "Tell me about Guatemala, Señor Laremos."

"Diego, please," he said, correcting her. "What would you like to know?"

"Anything."

He shrugged. "We have hopes for a better future, *señorita*, now that we have new leadership. But the guerrillas are still fighting the regime, and the *campanisos* are caught in the middle, as always. The warfare is sometimes very cruel. We are primarily an agricultural country, with an economy based on bananas and coffee. There is a sad lack of the things your people take for granted. Indoor plumbing, automobiles, adequate medical facilities—these things even the poorest of your people can expect, but here... Did you know, *señorita,* that the life expectancy in my country is only 50 years?"

She looked shocked. "Will things get better? Will the fighting stop?"

"We hope so. But in the meantime, those who wish to hold their land must have security. Mine is excellent. But many do not have the financial wherewithal to hire guards. I have a neighbor who gets government troops to go with him every afternoon to check his cattle and his holdings. He is afraid to go alone."

"I'll never grumble about paying income taxes again," Gabby said. "I guess we tend to take it for granted that we don't have to defend our property with guns."

"Perhaps someday we will be able to say the same thing."

Gabby was quiet for the rest of the trip, while J.D. and Laremos discussed things she couldn't begin to understand. Military terms. Logistics. She studied her taciturn employer with new eyes. There was more than he was telling her. It had something to do with the past he never discussed, and he was obviously reluctant to share any of it with her. Trust, again. At least he trusted her enough to let her handle the communications for this insane rescue attempt. If only he'd let those men go into the jungle and stay behind himself. Maybe she could talk him into it. It was a job for a professional soldier, not a lawyer. She closed her eyes and began to think up things to say, knowing in her heart that J.D. wasn't going to be swayed by any of them.

Chapter Four

Despite Gabby's unvoiced fears, they went through customs with no hitches, and minutes later were met by a man J.D. obviously knew.

The man was short and sandy blond, with a face like a railroad track and a slight figure. He was much older than the other two men, probably nearing fifty. He was wearing jungle fatigues with laced up boots. At his side was a holstered pistol; over his shoulder, a mean-looking rifle.

"Archer!" The short man chuckled, and they embraced roughly. "Damn, but I'm glad to see you, even under the circumstances. No sweat, *amigo*—we'll get Martina out of there. Apollo came like a shot when I told him what was on."

"How are you, First Shirt?" J.D. replied. "You've lost weight, I see."

"Well, I'm not exactly in the right profession for getting lazy, am I, Boss?" he asked Laremos, who agreed readily enough.

"Laremos said Apollo and Drago were here, but how about Chen?" J.D. asked.

The short man sighed. "He bought it in Lebanon, *amigo.*" He shrugged. "That's the way of it." His eyes were sad and had a faraway look. "It was how he'd have wanted it."

"Tough," J.D. said, agreeing. "Maps and radios, Shirt—we'll need those."

"All taken care of. Plus about twenty *vaqueros* for backup—the boss's men, and I trained 'em," he added with quiet pride.

"That's good enough for me."

"Shall we get under way?" Laremos asked, helping Gabby into a large car. He stood back to let J.D. slide in after her. They were joined by First Shirt, who drove, and another man with a rifle.

The topography was interesting. It reminded Gabby of photos of Caribbean islands, very lush and tropical and studded with palm trees. But after they drove for a while, it began to be mountainous. They passed a burned-out shell of what must have been a house, and Gabby shuddered.

"Diego," she said quietly, nodding toward the ruin, "the owners—did they escape?"

"No, *señorita*," he said.

She wrapped her arms around herself. J.D., noticing the gesture, pulled her closer. She let her head fall onto his shoulder quite naturally and closed her eyes while the men talked.

Laremos's *finca* was situated in a valley. The house seemed to be adobe or stucco, with large arches and an airy porch. It was only one story, and it spread out into a garden lush with tropical vegetation. She fell in love with it at first sight.

"You approve?" Laremos smiled, watching her with his dark, lazy eyes. "My father built it many years ago. The servants in the house are the children and grandchildren of those who came here with him, like most of my employees. The big landowners who hold the *fincas* provide employment for many people, and it is not so temporary as jobs in your country. Here the laborers serve the same household for generations."

They'd passed through a small village, and she remembered glimpses of dark-eyed, dark-skinned, barefooted children grouped around a big fountain, where women were drawing water in jugs. The apparent lack of modern conveniences made her grateful for her own life in Chicago.

She hadn't noticed anything unusual about the drive except that the small, dark man beside First Shirt had his rifle in his lap and kept watching the countryside. Now he stood beside the car, rifle ready, while the others went into the house.

It was dark for a moment until her eyes adjusted; then she began to see its interior. There were tiny statuettes, obviously Mayan, along with bowls of cacti, heavy wood furniture, and Indian blankets all around the big living room.

"Coffee?" Laremos asked. He clapped his hands and a small, dark woman about First Shirt's age came running with a smile on her face. *"Café, por favor, Carisa,"* he told the woman in rapid-fire Spanish.

She nodded and rushed away.

"Brandy, Archer?" he asked J.D.

"I don't drink these days," J.D. replied, dropping onto the comfortable sofa beside Gabby. "First Shirt, have you been able to get any intelligence out of the other camp?"

"Enough." The short, sandy-haired man nodded, also refusing the offer of brandy. "She isn't being mistreated, not yet, at least," he said, watching the younger man relax just a little. "They're holding her in the remains of a bunkhouse on a *finca* about six clicks away. They aren't well armed—just some AK-47s and grenades, no heavy stuff. They don't have an RPG-7 between them."

"What is a click? And what's an RPG?" Gabby asked.

"A click is a kilometer. An RPG is a rocket launcher, Russian made," J.D. explained. "It makes big holes in things."

"Like tanks and aircraft and buildings," First Shirt added. "You must be Gabby. I've heard a lot about you."

She was taken aback. Everybody seemed to know about her, but she'd never heard of any of these people. She glanced at J.D.

"So I brag about you a little," he said defensively.

"To everybody but me," she returned. "You never even pat me on the head and tell me I've done a good job."

"Remind me later," he said with a slow smile.

"Could I freshen up?" Gabby asked.

"Of course! Carisa!" Laremos called.

The Latin woman entered with a tray of coffee, and he spoke to her again in Spanish.

"Sí, señor," Carisa murmured.

"I've asked her to show you your room," Laremos explained. "Archer, you might like to take the bags and go with them. Then we can talk."

"Suits me." J.D. picked up the cases and followed Gabby and the serving woman down the hall.

The room had a huge double bed. It was the first thing Gabby noticed, and she felt herself go hot all over, especially when Carisa left and she was alone with J.D.

He closed the door deliberately and watched her fiddle with her cosmetic case as she set it down on the dresser.

"Gabby."

She put down a bottle of makeup and turned.

He moved just in front of her and framed her small face in his hands. "I don't want you out of my sight any more than you have to be. Laremos is charming, but there are things about him you don't know. About all these men."

"Including you, Mr. Brettman?" she asked gently, searching his eyes. "Especially you?"

He drew in a slow breath. "What do you want to know?"

"You were one of them, weren't you, J.D.?" she asked quietly. "They're more than old friends. They're old comrades-in-arms.''

"I wondered when you'd guess," he murmured. His eyes darkened. "Does it matter?"

She frowned. "I don't understand. Why should the fact that you served in the Special Forces with them matter?"

He seemed torn between speech and silence. He drew in a breath and rammed his hands in his pockets. "You don't know about the years before you met me, Gabby."

"Nobody does. It has something to do with trust, doesn't it?"

He met her searching green eyes squarely. "Yes. A lot. I've lived by hard rules for a long time. I've trusted no one, because it could have meant my life. These men—First Shirt and Laremos and the rest—I know I can trust them, because under fire they never failed me. Laremos, maybe once—that's one reason I brought you along. Against my better judgment," he added dryly. "I'm still not sure I could live with myself if anything happened to you here."

"And that's why you want me in the same room with you?" she probed delicately.

"Not quite," he admitted, watching her. "I want you in the same room because I've dreamed of holding you in my arms all night. I won't make any blatant passes at you, Gabby, but the feel of you in the bed will light up my darkness in ways I can't explain to you."

She felt her heart hammering. He made it sound wildly erotic, to be held close to that massive body all night long, to go to sleep in his arms. Her breath caught in her throat; her eyes looked up into his and her blood surged in her veins.

His fingers moved down to her throat, stroking it with a deliberately sensuous lightness. "Is your blood running as hot as mine is right now?" he asked under his breath. "Does your body want the feel of mine against it?"

He bent and tilted her face up to his, so that he could watch her expression. His mouth opened as it brushed against hers.

"Stand very still," he whispered, opening her mouth with his. "Very, very still..."

She gasped as his hard, moist lips began to merge with her own. She tasted him, actually tasted the essence of him, as he built the intensity of the kiss. His hands moved down her back, bringing her torso against his and letting her soft breasts crush against the hardness of his chest. His teeth nipped roughly at her mouth as he drew slowly away. His eyes were blazing—fierce and passionate and hungry.

"I like it hard," he said under his breath. "Will I frighten you?"

She barely managed to shake her head before he bent again. This time it was a tempest, not the slight breeze of before. He lifted her in his hard arms and she felt the heat in him as his mouth opened wide. She felt his tongue go inside her mouth in a fencing motion that made her feel hot all over and dragged a smothered moan from her throat.

She was trembling, and her body couldn't seem to get close enough to his. She clung to him, trying to weld herself to him, but before she could move, he was putting her on her feet. His eyes blazed wildly in his pale face.

"No more of that," he said heavily. He freed her abruptly, and the blood rushed back into her upper arms, making her aware of the pressure of his unconscious hold on her. "My God, you were trembling all over."

She felt naked under his glittering gaze. She'd never been vulnerable like that with anyone, but to have it happen with J.D. was terrifying.

"I feel funny," she said with a shaky laugh.

"Do you?" He took a deep breath and drew her head to his shoulder. "I'm sorry. I'm sorry, Gabby. I'm not used to virgins."

"That never happened to me before." She hadn't meant to confess it, but the words came tumbling out involuntarily.

"Yes, I felt that," he murmured. His hands, tangled in her hair, gently drew her closer to him so that her cheek rested against his chest. "Gabby, do you know what I'd like to do? I'd like to take off my shirt and feel your cheek against my skin, your lips on my body..." He groaned and suddenly pushed her away, turning on his heel. He seemed to go rigid, and his hands reached blindly for a cigarette while Gabby stood behind him and ached for what he'd just described.

"How long have we worked together...two years?" he asked in an odd tone. "And we spend two days posing as lovers and this happens. Maybe bringing you along wasn't such a good idea."

"You said you needed me," she reminded him.

He pulled out another cigarette and lit it, handing it to her with an oddly apologetic look. "It will steady you," he said gently. "Gabby, just don't tempt me, all right?"

"Do what?" she asked blankly, looking up at him with dazed eyes.

"Damn!" he growled and then sighed. "Gabby, what I'm trying to say is, let's not get emotional."

"You're the one who's cursing, counselor, not me," she reminded him coldly. "And I didn't start kissing you!"

"You helped," he reminded her, his eyes narrow. "You'd be a joy to initiate."

"I am not sleeping with you!"

His knuckles brushed her mouth, silencing her. "I was teasing. I won't do anything to you that you'll regret, Gabby, that's a promise. No sex."

She swallowed. "You scare me."

"Why?"

"Because of the way you make me feel," she confessed. "I didn't expect it."

"Neither did I. You're a heady wine, honey. One I don't dare drink much of." He lifted his hand to her hair. "You could be habit-forming to a man like me, who's been alone too long."

"Maybe I'd better resign when we get back..." she began, shaken as much by what she was feeling as by what he was telling her.

"No!" he said curtly. His fingers caught the nape of her neck and held on. "No. This is all just a moment out of time, Gabby. It's no reason to start getting panicky. Besides," he added heavily, "there's still Martina. And God only knows how this will turn out."

She went icy cold. "Jacob, please don't go with the others."

"I have to," he said simply.

"You could get killed," she said.

He nodded. "That could happen. But Martina is all I have in the world, the only person I've ever loved. I can't turn my back on her, not now. I could never call myself a man again."

What could she say to that? He touched her cheek lightly and left her alone in the room. She watched the door close with a sense of utter disaster. It didn't help that she was beginning to understand why she trembled so violently at his touch.

J.D. had always disturbed her, from the very first. But she'd assumed that it was because of the kind of man he was. Now, she didn't know. Just looking at him made her ache. And he'd kissed her...how he'd kissed her! As if he were hungry for her, for her alone.

She shook herself. Probably he just needed a woman and she was handy. He'd said not to get herself involved, and she wasn't going to. Just because she was all excited at the prospect of being part of a covert operation, that was no reason to go overboard for J.D.

She wondered at the way he'd reacted when she'd asked if he had been one of the group before. Didn't he remember that he'd told her he'd served in the Special Forces?

It was fifteen minutes before she rejoined the men, wearing jeans and a loose pullover top and boots. J.D. studied her long and hard, his eyes clearly approving the modest gear.

She stared back at him. He seemed like a different man, sitting there in jungle fatigues and holding some small weapon in his big hands.

"The Uzi," he told her when she approached and stared at the miniature machine gun curiously. "It holds a thirty-shot magazine."

"And what's that?" she asked, nodding toward a nasty-looking oversize rifle with a long torpedo-like thing on a stick near it.

"An RPG-7 rocket launcher."

"Is that Gabby?" a short black man asked, grinning at her.

"That's Gabby." J.D. chuckled. "Honey, this is Drago, one of the best explosives men this side of nuclear war. And over in the corner, being antisocial, is Apollo. He's the scrounger. What we need, he gets."

She nodded toward the corner, where a second black man stood. That one was tall and slender, whereas Drago was chunky.

"Hey, Gabby," Apollo said without looking up.

"Does everybody know my name?" she burst out, exasperated.

"Afraid so," First Shirt volunteered, laughing. "Didn't you know Archer was a blabbermouth?"

She stared at her boss. "Well, I sure do now," she exclaimed.

"Come here, Gabby, and let me show you how to work the radio," Laremos offered, starting to rise.

"My job," J.D. said in a tone of voice that made Laremos sit back down.

"But of course." Laremos grinned, not offended at all.

Gabby followed the big man out of the room to the communications room, where

Laremos had a computer and several radios.

"J.D...." she began.

He closed the door and glared down at her. "He hurt a woman once. Badly. Can you read between the lines, or are you naïve enough that I have to spell it out in words of one syllable?"

She drew in a steadying breath. "I'm sorry, J.D. You'll just have to make allowances for my stupidity. I'm a small-town Texas girl. Where I come from, men are different."

"Yes, I know. You aren't used to this kind of group."

She looked up. "No. But they seem to be nice people. J.D., it just dawned on me that you must trust me a lot to bring me here," she murmured.

"There isn't anyone I trust more," he said in a deep, rough tone. "Didn't you know?"

He stared into her eyes until she felt the trembling come back, and something wild darkened his own before he turned away and got it under control.

"We'd better get to it," he said tautly. "And when we go back out there, for God's sake, don't say or do anything to encourage Laremos, you understand? He's a friend of mine, but I'd kill him in a second if he touched you."

The violence in him made her eyes widen with shock. He glanced at her, his face hard, and she knew she was seeing the man without the mask for the first time. He looked as ruthless as any one of those men in the other room and she realized with a start that he was.

"I'm territorial," he said gruffly. "What I have, I hold, and for the duration of this trip, you belong to me. Enough said?"

"Enough said, Jacob," she replied, her voice unconsciously soft.

His face tautened. "I'd like to hear you say my name in bed, Gabby," he breathed, moving close. "I'd like to hear you scream it..."

"Jacob!" she gasped as he bent and took her mouth.

She moaned helplessly as he folded her into his tall, powerful form, letting her feel for the first time the involuntary rigidity of his body in desire.

He lifted his lips from hers and looked into her wide eyes, and he nodded. "Yes, it happens to me just as it happens to other men," he said in a rough tone. "Are you shocked? Haven't you ever been this close to a hungry man?"

"No, Jacob, I haven't," she managed unsteadily.

That seemed to calm him a little, but his eyes were still stormy. He let her move away, just enough to satisfy her modesty.

"Are you frightened?" he asked.

"You're very strong," she said, searching his face. "I know you wouldn't force me, but what if...?"

"I've had a lot of practice at curbing my appetites, Gabby," he murmured. He brushed the hair away from her cheeks. "I won't lose my head, even with you.

"Let me show you," he whispered, and she felt his mouth beside hers, touching, moving away, teasing, until she turned her head just a fraction of an inch and opened it to the slow, sweet possession of his lips.

She could barely breathe, and it was heaven as his arms came around her, as his mouth spoke to her in a wild, nonverbal way. The opening of the door was a shattering disappointment.

"Excuse me"—Laremos chuckled—"but you were so long, I thought you might be having trouble."

"I am," J.D. said in a voice husky with emotion, "but not the kind you thought."

"As I see. Here, let me go over the sequence with you and discuss the frequencies—they are different from the ones you are familiar with, no doubt," he said, sitting down in front of the equipment.

Gabby brushed back her hair and tried not to look at J.D. She tried not to think about the long night ahead, when she'd lie in his arms in that big bed and have to keep from begging him to do what they both wanted.

The radio wasn't difficult at all. It took only minutes to learn the routine. It was the code words that took longest. She made a list and walked around the house memorizing it while the men talked in the spacious living room. At the dinner table, she was still going over it.

Only Laremos, J.D., and Gabby ate together at the table. The others carried their plates away.

"They're still antisocial, I see," J.D. murmured over his food.

"Old habits." Laremos glanced at Gabby. "And I think they do not want to disillusion this one, who looks at them with such soft eyes."

"I didn't embarrass them, did I?" she asked, contrite.

"No," J.D. said. "I think you flattered them. They aren't used to all that rapt attention." He chuckled.

"How did they come to be mercenaries?" she asked softly. "If you can tell me, I mean. I don't want to invade anyone's privacy."

"Well, Shirt was in the Special Forces, like I was," J.D. said, pausing over the sentence, as if he was choosing his words carefully. "After he got out of the service, he couldn't find anything he liked to do except police work, and he wasn't making enough to pay the bills. He had a contact in the mercenary network and he asked some questions. He was good with the standard underworld weapons and something of a small-arms expert. He found work.''

"And Apollo?"

"Apollo started out as an M.P. He was accused of a crime he didn't commit, and there were some racial overtones." J.D. shrugged. "He wasn't getting any justice, so he ran for it and wound up in Central America. He's been down here ever since."

"He can't clear himself?" she asked.

"I expect I'll end up defending him one of these days," he told her with a quiet smile. "In fact, I can almost guarantee it. I'll win, too."

"I wouldn't doubt that," she murmured, tongue in cheek.

"How long have you worked with this bad-tempered one, Señorita Gabby?" Laremos asked.

"A little over two years," she told him, glancing at J.D. "It's been an education. I've learned that if you shout loudly enough, you can get most anything you want."

"He shouts at you?"

"I wouldn't dare," J.D. murmured with a grin. "The first time I tried, she heaved a paperweight at my head."

"I did not," she protested. "I threw it at your door!"

"Which I opened at the wrong time," he continued. "Fortunately, I have good reflexes."

"You will need them tomorrow, I fear," Laremos told him. "The terrorists will not make things easy for us."

"True," J.D. said as he finished his coffee. "But we have the element of surprise on our side."

"That is so."

"And now, we'd better go over the maps again. I want to be sure I know the terrain before we set out in the morning."

Gabby went on to bed, feeling definitely in the way. She took a quick bath and settled in on one side of the big double bed, wearing the long, very modest nightgown she'd brought along. Unfortunately, the material was thin, but perhaps J.D. would be too busy with his thoughts to notice.

She lay there trying to stumble through a Guatemalan newspaper, but she couldn't concentrate. She tingled all over, thinking of the long night ahead, of spending it lying in J.D.'s arms. Had he really meant that? Or had it just been something to tease her with? And what if he did hold her in his arms all night—would she be able to resist tempting him beyond his control?

She tossed the newspaper onto the floor and wrapped her arms around her knees, staring apprehensively at the door. Her long hair hung softly around her shoulders, and she brushed strands of it away from her face. She wanted him. There was no use denying that she did. But if she gave in, if she tempted him too far, what would she have? One single night to remember, and it would be the end of her job. J.D. didn't want any kind of permanent relationship with a woman, and she'd do well to keep her head. He was worried about his sister, justifiably nervous about tomorrow's foray into the jungle, and he might do something insane if she pushed him.

But for just a moment she thought how it would be, to feel his hair-roughened skin against every inch of her, to let him touch her as he'd no doubt touched other women. She sighed huskily. He'd be gentle, she knew that, and patient. He'd make of it such a tender initiation that it would surpass her wildest dreams of belonging to a man. But it would cheapen what she was beginning to feel for him, and it would do no good for his opinion of her. She attracted him because she was a virgin, untouched. And if she gave herself to him, she wouldn't be that any-more. It was even possible that he'd hold her in contempt for joining the ranks of his lovers.

With a weary moan, she turned out the light and burrowed under the covers. It was a lovely dream, anyway, she told herself, and closed her eyes.

She hadn't meant to go to sleep so soon, but the first thing she knew the dawn light was streaming in through the windows, bringing her wide awake.

Sleepily she stretched, and became suddenly aware of where she was. She sat up, eyes wide, and looked around for J.D. It took only a second to find him. He was standing at the window, his profile to her, looking out. And he didn't have a stitch of clothing on his body.

Her eyes were riveted on him. She'd seen men without clothes. These days, with all the explicit films, it was impossible to avoid nudity. But she'd never seen a nude man close up, like this. And she imagined that J.D. would please even the eyes of an experienced woman.

He was all powerful muscle, with dark shadows of hair feathering every inch of him. His legs were long and muscular, his hips narrow, his stomach flat. His chest was broad and bronzed and a wedge of thick black hair curled over it. She stared at him helplessly, unashamedly—until she happened to look up and saw him watching her.

Her lips trembled as she tried to speak, but she couldn't get anything out.

"It's all right," he said quietly. "If I'd found you in the same condition, I'd be staring just as hard. There's nothing to be embarrassed about.

"I don't wear pajamas," he murmured with an amused look. "I expected to be awake before you were. It was a hot night."

"Yes," she managed, choking.

He moved back toward the bed, and she sat there frozen, unable to make even the pretense of looking the other way. It didn't seem to bother him at all. He bent down, catching her by the arms, and dragged her out of the bed and against his body.

He laughed deep in his throat, the sound of it predatory, primitive. "Touch me," he dared her. His hands caught hers and ran them over his sleek hips, up his spine, and around to the matted tangle of hair over his warm chest.

Her breath was trapped somewhere beneath her ribs, and her fingers burrowed into the crisp hair over his heart.

"Yes, you like it, don't you?" he asked in a voice like rough velvet, his eyes narrow and black and hot on her face. "But not half as much as I do. I've dreamed about this, night after endless night, about how your hands would feel touching me. What do I look like to those innocent eyes, Gabby? Do I frighten you...please you? Which?"

She was drunk with the feel of him, the smell of him. Her hands roamed over his chest, his rib cage. With a long sigh she leaned her forehead on his collarbone. "You please me," she whispered. "Can't you tell? Oh, Jacob...!" Her hands pressed harder, more urgently. "Jacob, I want to do such shameless things."

"Such as?" he asked in a whisper. "Such as, Gabby?" He covered her hands with his own and she felt their faint tremor. "I won't hurt you. Do whatever you want to do."

It wasn't fair that he should have such power over her, she thought dazedly. She was too intoxicated, too hungry, to listen to the cool voice of reason. Her hands smoothed over his chest, around his back, and with an instinct she didn't even know she had, her mouth opened and pressed against the center of his chest.

He groaned harshly, shocking her. She lifted wide, curious eyes to his.

"I like it," he whispered huskily. "Do it again."

She moved closer, and his hands caught her head, guiding her mouth to the places he wanted it, while the silence lengthened and grew around them and J.D.'s breath came raggedly and in gasps. She learned so much about him all at once. That she drove him wild when she rubbed her cheek across his taut nipples, that he liked the curl of her tongue around the tangled hair. That she could nip him gently with her teeth and make him go rigid. That he wanted her badly enough to tremble.

"This isn't fair, Jacob," she whispered shakily, "I'm making you miserable, I'm..."

His thumb pressed across her mouth. His face looked strained, but his eyes were blazing. "I want it," he whispered roughly.

"But I'm hurting you," she said achingly.

"Such a sweet hurt," he whispered, bending. "So sweet, so beautiful...let me make you ache like this, Gabby. I won't seduce you, I promise I won't, but let me touch you..."

His hand moved between them and lightly touched her breast. The gown was thin, and his fingers were warm, and the sudden intimacy was shocking and pleasurable, all at once.

She gasped and instinctively caught his fingers. He lifted his head and looked down, and he smiled.

"Habit?" he whispered.

Her fingers lingered on his hairy wrist. "I . . . I haven't ever let . . ." she began.

"You'll let me." His face nuzzled hers, his cheek rubbed gently against hers and he found her mouth, cherishing it with a whispery soft pressure that was wildly exciting.

And all the while, his fingers were shaping, probing, lightly brushing until they caused a helpless reaction in her body. He drew the gown tightly around her breasts and lifted his head.

"Look," he said softly, directing her eyes down to the rigid peaks outlined under the gown. "Do you know what it means, what your body tells me when that happens?"

Her lips opened as she tried to breathe. "It means . . . that I want you," she whispered back.

"Yes." He brushed her lips apart with his, tracing the line of them with his tongue. His teeth caught her upper one and nibbled gently, tugging it, smiling as she reached up to do the same thing to his.

"Jacob," she whispered. Her hands crept around his neck. "Jacob..." She arched and pressed herself to him, and froze, shocked at what his taut body was telling hers.

"Body language," he whispered, coaxing her mouth open again. "Now listen. I'm going to strip you out of that gown and hold you to me, just for a second, and then I'm going to get the hell out of here before I go crazy. I don't know what we'll be walking into today. I want one perfect memory to take with me, you understand?"

She did. Because it was just dawning on her that she was in love with him. Why else would she be doing this?

She felt his hands unbuttoning the garment and she looked up because she wanted to see his face, she wanted to remember always the expression on it. In case anything happened . . .

He eased the gown off her shoulders and she felt it suddenly drop to the floor. She felt the whisper of the breeze against her bare skin. J.D.'s eyes blazed as he looked down at her body. And then he drew her to him, and she felt herself go rigid all over.

"I won't live long enough to forget how this feels," he whispered. "Now kiss me, one last time."

And she did, with all her heart and soul, without a single inhibition. And her arms held him and they fused together in a silence gone mad with tangible hunger.

He groaned as if he were being tortured and his arms hurt her, his lips hurt, his tongue thrust into her mouth in a deliciously fierce invasion. Finally he drew back, shaking, and put her from him.

He bent, picked up the nightgown, and gently drew it back on her without a single word.

"Worth dying for," he whispered, studying her luminous eyes, her swollen mouth, her flushed cheeks. "God, you're sweet."

"Jacob, don't go out there," she pleaded.

"I have to." He bent and retrieved his clothes from a chair where he must have flung them the night before and began to dress.

"But you're a lawyer," she persisted. She wiped away a tear and sat down heavily on the side of the bed, her green eyes wide and frightened. "You aren't a soldier."

"But I was, honey," he said as he tugged on his jungle fatigues. He turned, buttoning the shirt, his eyes dark and mysterious as they searched hers. "You still haven't worked it out, have you, Gabby?"

"Worked what out?"

He tucked in the shirt. "I served only three years in the Special Forces. I joined when I was eighteen."

She was trying to do mathematics with a mind still drugged by pleasure. "You were twenty-one when you got out."

"Yes. But I didn't start studying for my degree until I was twenty-five."

She stared at him, uncomprehending. "That means...you did something else with those four years."

"Yes." He met her searching gaze levelly. "I was a mercenary. I led First Shirt and the others for the better part of four years, in some of the nastiest little uprisings in the civilized world."

Chapter Five

Gabby stared at him as if she'd never seen him before. J.D., a mercenary? One of those men who hired out to fight wars, who risked their lives daily?

"Are you shocked, honey?" he asked, his eyes searching, his stance challenging.

Her lips parted. "I never realized... you said you served with them, but I never realized... I thought you meant in the Special Forces."

"I was going to let you go on thinking that, too," he said. "But maybe it's better to get it out into the open."

Her eyes went over him, looking for scars, for changes. She'd noticed the tiny white lines on his stomach and chest, partially hidden by the hair, but until now it hadn't dawned on her what they were.

"You have scars," she began hesitantly.

"A hell of a lot of them," he said. "Do you want to hear it all, Gabby?"

"Yes."

He rammed his hands into his pockets and went to stare out of the window, as if it was easier to talk when he didn't look at her. "I stayed in the service because it meant I made enough to keep Martina in a boarding school. We had no relatives, you see. Mama was gone." He shrugged. "But when I got out of the service, I couldn't get a job that paid enough to get Martina through school. I wasn't trained for much except combat." He fumbled in his pocket for a cigarette and lit it. "I thought I'd given this up until the kidnapping," he said absently, holding the cigarette to his lips. He drew in and blew out a cloud of smoke. "Well, Shirt was recruiting, and he knew I was in trouble. He offered me a job. I took it. I spent the next four years globe-trotting with my crossbow and my Uzi. I made money, and I put it in foreign banks. But I got too confident and too careless, and I got shot to pieces.''

She held her breath, waiting for him to continue.

''I spent weeks in a hospital. My lungs collapsed from shrapnel and they thought I was going to die. But I lived through it. When I got out, I realized that there was only one way I could go from there, and it was straight downhill. So I told Shirt I was quitting.'' He laughed mirthlessly. ''But first I went on one last mission, just to prove to myself that I still had the guts. And I came out of that one without a scratch. I came back to the States afterward. I figured that someday the guys I'd served with might need a lawyer, and I needed a profession. So I got a job and went to school at night.''

''You aren't a fugitive?'' she asked.

''No. In one or two countries, perhaps, if I were recognized. But not in the States.'' He turned, studying her through narrowed eyes. ''That's why I guard my past so meticulously, Gabby. And it's why I don't like reporters. I'm not ashamed of the old life. But I don't like being reminded of it too often."

"Do you miss it?" she asked, probing gently.

He sighed. "Yes. Part of me does. Life is so precious when you've touched death, Gabby. You become alive in a way I can't explain to you. Life is pretty damned tame afterward."

"This is why you came after Martina, isn't it, Jacob?" she asked, fitting the puzzle pieces together. "Because you knew that you and the group could succeed where a larger group might fail."

"We're the only chance she has, honey," he said quietly. "In Italy I might have stayed out of it. But down here... the government has its hands full just trying to keep the economy from failing, and there are other factions fighting for control as well. Besides all that, damn it, she's my sister. She's all I've got."

That hurt. He might want Gabby, but he didn't care about her. He'd made that perfectly clear. She lowered her eyes to the skirt of her nightgown.

"Yes, I can understand that," she said in a subdued tone.

"I had a long talk with Laremos last night," he said. "I told him that if he touched you, I'd kill him. You'll be safe here."

Her head jerked up. "I'm not afraid for myself," she said. "Only for you and the others."

"We're a good team," he said. "The way you and I have been for the past two years. Do you want to quit now, Gabby? Are you disillusioned?"

He sounded coldly sarcastic. He lifted the cigarette to his lips with a short laugh.

"Are you firing me?" she threw back, angered by the unexpected and unwarranted attack.

"No. If you leave, it's up to you."

"I'll think about it," she said.

He crushed out his cigarette in an ashtray. "You'd better get dressed. I want to go over those codes with you one last time before we get under way."

"Yes, of course," she murmured. She got up and went to find her clothes. Before she could turn around, the door opened and he'd gone out.

She got dressed and sat down on the bed and cried. To go from dream to nightmare in such a short space of time was anguish. And the worst thing was that she didn't even know what had happened.

It didn't matter to her that he'd been a soldier of fortune, she thought miserably. How could it, when she loved him?

Loved him. Her eyes pictured him, dark and solemn and strong, and a surge of warmth swept over her like fire. She would have followed him through that jungle on her knees without a single complaint. But despite his obvious hunger for her, he didn't want anything emotional between them. He'd pretty well spelled that out for her. Martina was the only person on earth he loved or would love, and he'd said so. What he felt for Gabby was purely physical, something he couldn't help. She was a virgin and she excited him. He wanted her, but that was all. And he could have had her that morning, without a protest on her part. He must have known it too. But he hadn't taken her, because he was strong. He didn't want her getting involved with him, so he'd told her all about his past.

That was the final blow, that he'd shared his past with her, only to put a wall between them. She hid her face in her hands and tried to hold back the tears. How was she going to manage to work with him day after day now, when he couldn't help but see how she felt?

But that wasn't the worst of it. He was going out into the jungle after kidnappers who could kill him. Her heart froze in her chest. She couldn't stop him. All she could do was sit there and pray for him.

All the pleas in the world wouldn't hold him back, not when Martina's life hung in the balance. If there was a chance of any kind, he would take it. But if he died . . . oh, God, if he died, there would be nothing of worth left in Gabby's life. Tears welled up in her soft green eyes as she tried to imagine a world without him. She wanted to go with him, to risk her life at his side, to die with him if that was what lay in store. But even as she thought it, she knew that nothing would convince him to take her along. He might not love her, but he was fiercely protective of her. He wouldn't allow her to risk her life. And she couldn't fight him.

With a resigned sigh, she got up, combed her hair, and went into the living room where the men were assembled. It took the last ounce of courage she possessed to smile at them. She couldn't meet J.D.'s searching gaze at all. It would cut her to the quick to see indifference in his eyes.

There was a new face in the room. It belonged to a dark, lithe man with pale blue eyes.

"Semson," J.D. told her, indicating the newcomer. "He's been out scouting for the past day or so."

"Gabby?" the new man murmured and grinned at her. "How do you stand working for this dude?"

She smiled wanly. "Oh, it has its moments," she confessed, but she didn't look at J.D. as she said it.

J.D. had picked up an automatic weapon something like a machine gun and slung it over his shoulder, but he was carrying the crossbow. Gabby stared pointedly at it and suddenly realized what it was for.

She looked up, and he seemed to read the thought in her mind.

He nodded. "Sentries," he said, confirming her suspicions. "If there are any."

She felt her throat go dry. She'd never been in a situation like this, and she could have kicked herself for coming along. It was one thing to watch an operation like this in a fictional TV show. But to realize that any one of these men, especially J.D., might never come back from the rescue attempt . . . that was altogether different.

"Hey, Gabby, don't look so grim," Apollo chided. "I won't let this big turkey get himself hurt."

Gabby laughed despite herself. "Thanks, Apollo," she said. "I've gotten kind of used to him."

"That works both ways. Laremos, take care of her," J.D. told the other man.

Laremos nodded. "Be assured that I will. Now, shall we double-check our coordinates and codes?"

They did, and Gabby felt her palms sweating as she rattled off the codes from memory. She knew how important they were, and that made her more nervous than ever.

"Calm down," J.D. said quietly. "You're okay."

She smiled for him. "Sure. You guys take it easy out there, okay?"

"We're sort of used to this kind of thing," First Shirt said with a wink. "Okay, guys. Hit it."

And just that quickly, they left. Gabby stood at the front door with her wide, unblinking gaze riveted on J.D.'s broad back. He didn't turn or say anything to her. It hurt terribly.

"How long will it take them to get there, Diego?" she asked the man at her side.

"At least an hour or two, Gabby," he replied. "The terrain is rugged, and they require much stealth."

She glanced up to see that his eyes were concerned. "Are you worried?"

"Of course not," he said, but he was lying and she knew it. His smile didn't reach his eyes.

"I'll get a cup of coffee, if I may, and sit beside the receiver."

He studied her closely. "Archer—you care very much for him."

"Yes," she said simply.

"Will you believe me if I tell you that of all the men I have known, he is the most capable under fire?" he said gently. "I have seen him come back from the grave. And their opponents have traveled far, *señorita*, and are already decimated in numbers. They will not expect such an attack here. We have seen to it that their intelligence is distorted."

"But what if something goes wrong?" she burst out.

He sighed. "Then it is in the hands of God, is it not?"

She thought about that for the next three hours, pacing and sweating and worried out of her mind.

"Shouldn't we have heard something?" she asked finally, her face contorted with fear.

Laremos frowned. "It is rugged terrain," he reiterated.

"Yes, but . . . listen!"

The radio broke its silence, and Gabby made a dive for it. She gave the correct identification and waited.

"Panther to Red Rover," J.D.'s voice said curtly. "Bravo. Tango in ten. Out."

She keyed the mike. "Red Rover here. Alpha. Omega. Out."

The code words meant that the group had arrived undetected and would make their play in ten minutes. She'd radioed back that the message was understood and that there was no new intelligence to convey.

She looked up at Laremos, feeling her heart go wild as she realized how close the danger was. "Ten minutes," she said.

"The waiting is the hardest, is it not?" he asked quietly. "I will have Carisa fix us another pot of coffee."

He strode away, and Gabby prayed and chewed her nails and stared at the microphone as if it held the key to salvation.

Long, agonizing minutes later, the static came again. "Panther to Red Rover," J.D.

said tightly, as gunfire and an explosion of some sort sounded in the background. "Charlie Tango! Heat up the coffee. Out!"

Her fingers trembled as she returned, "Red Rover to Panther. Bravo. Omega. Out!"

She'd just signed off when Laremos came tearing into the room, eyes flashing.

"Raise them quickly! One of my men just reported that he's sighted a large guerrilla force moving toward Archer's position!"

She grabbed the mike. "Red Rover to Panther. Red Rover to Panther. Come in, Panther!"

But there was no answer. Frantically she tried again and again, and still there was no answer. Her frightened eyes went to Laremos.

"They must be under fire," he said heavily, "or they would answer. We can only pray that they spot the newcomers in time."

She stared at the mike, hating it. Her cold fingers keyed it again, and again she gave the message. There was no answer.

Her mind went wild. J.D., answer me, she pleaded silently. I can't lose you now, I can't!

As if he heard her, somewhere miles away, the radio blared. "Red Rover, we're cut off by guerrillas, lots of them," J.D. said sharply. "Going into the jungle coordinates two clicks from position Delta. Gabby, get the hell out of there, they're heading in your direction . . . !"

The radio went dead. Gabby stared at it helplessly and then at Laremos.

"Madre de Dios," he breathed. "I should have realized . . . Carisa!" he yelled. A stream of Spanish followed, and Laremos grabbed one of the weapons J.D. had called an AK-47. He thrust it into Gabby's numbed fingers.

"Carry it. I will teach you to use it when I must," he said curtly. "Come, there is no time. Aquilas!" he yelled, and the short man who'd driven in from the airport with them came running in. There was another stream of Spanish.

"My men will cover us," Laremos said curtly. "We must hurry. The guerrillas will not care who are terrorists and who are not, they will cut us down regardless. Aquilas says the government troops are not too far behind. But we cannot involve them." His wary eyes sought hers. "You understand?"

"Because of the rescue," she said, smiling wanly. "It's all right, *señor*. Just, please, get me to J.D."

He looked at her searchingly. "I understand. But do not underestimate the group, *señorita*. We were once... quite something."

He led her out of the house, and together they headed quickly into the jungle. She carried the heavy weapon with no real sense of its weight and no earthly idea of how to use it. As she followed Laremos through dense undergrowth at a breakneck pace, she wondered what her mother back home in Lytle, Texas, would think if she knew where her only daughter was.

"Quick, get down," Laremos hissed, pushing her under the dense foliage and cautioning her to be quiet.

She froze, her heart pounding painfully in her chest. She felt weak all over. What would

happen if they were seen? She couldn't fire
the weapon, she didn't know how! Her eyes
felt as if they were going to pop out of her
head, and she wished she were with J.D.
Laremos would do his best, but if she had to
die, she wanted to be with Jacob when it
happened. Her eyes closed and she prayed
silently while sweat poured down her cheeks.

There was a wild thrashing nearby, and
she had a glimpse of ragged-looking men
with rifles, wearing some sort of soldiers'
garb. She knew without being told that they
were the guerrillas Laremos had spoken
about. They were muttering among themselves, but they didn't seem to be looking for
anyone. They were joking and laughing,
their weapons hung over their shoulders as
they trailed through the jungle.

Gabby bit almost through her lower lip as
she studied the weapons they were carrying.
She could feel terror in her throat, stran-
gling her. What if they were spotted? There
were worse things than being killed, especially for a woman, and she remembered
what she'd read about this part of the world.

Her eyes closed. The bravery she'd thought she had was nowhere to be found.

It seemed to take forever for the men to march out of sight and finally out of earshot.

"Courage," Laremos whispered. "We will wait just another minute and then proceed."

"We can't go back to your *finca?*" she whispered back, hating her own cowardice.

He shook his head. "This is only a small part of the main force. Unless I am badly mistaken, the rest are camped at my *finca.*" He shrugged. "The government troops will come and drive them out. But for the meantime, we have little choice. We either try to join our comrades or risk being killed."

"I'm much too young to die," she told him with a quiet smile. "How do I shoot this thing if I have to?"

He showed her, quickly and efficiently, and she felt a little more secure as they started out again. But her eyes darted every which way, and she was so afraid that she could taste the fear in her mouth. Death seemed to lurk behind every tree.

She was learning something about courage. It wasn't being unafraid. It was being stubborn.

It was slow going. Laremos had a pedometer, a compass, and a map, and he was using all three. They had been walking for over an hour when suddenly gunfire erupted all around them.

"Oh, my God," Gabby squealed, dropping down with her hands over her head, the AK-47 falling to the ground.

"Don't panic," Laremos said tautly as he came down beside her. "Listen."

She heard bullets whizzing, but Laremos was grinning!

"What . . . ?" she tried to ask, gathering enough courage to grab her weapon and hold onto it with cold fingers.

"The Uzi," he whispered. "I know the sound, oh, so well, *señorita*," he said with a grin. He moved behind a tree and peered out into the jungle. All at once, he stood up. "Archer!" he yelled. "Here!"

Then there was a flurry of wild movement, crashing sounds, gunfire, and explosions, and in the middle of it came J.D., with a small, dark-haired woman under one arm and the Uzi under the other. Around him, Shirt and Apollo and Semson and Drago were covering each other and firing on the run as they joined Laremos and Gabby.

"Martina, Gabby," J.D. said as he piled in with them and let go of his sister. "Okay, honey?" he asked Gabby with a quick glance.

"Fine, now," she whispered shakily, clutching the weapon.

"They're right on our tails," J.D. said. "Apollo, got any of that C-4 left?" he yelled.

"Working on it right now, big man," came the reply. "Just enough to make a big splash. We'll have to draw them in."

"Tell me when," J.D. called back.

"The guerrillas have taken my *finca*," Laremos said. "We barely escaped in time."

"I'm sorry about that," J.D. said as he reloaded the small automatic weapon.

"Are you both all right?" Gabby asked J.D. in a quavering voice as she crawled over to Martina and clutched the frightened woman's hand.

"A few scratches, but we'll make it," he returned, but his eyes were fierce and tormented as they searched Gabby's face. "How about you?"

"I'm learning to be a crack shot," she replied with a nervous laugh. "Laremos even told me how to cock this thing."

"If you have to fire it," J.D. said intently, "be sure you brace it hard against your shoulder so that the recoil doesn't break a bone. Take a breath, let half of it out, and squeeze the trigger, don't jerk it."

"I'll be a natural," Gabby told him, but she was trembling.

"I wish I could help," Martina whispered shakily. "But I'm so tired . . . !"

"God knows you've reason to be," J.D. said. He ruffled her hair. "But you're a trooper, Sis."

She managed a smile for him. "Like my big brother. I knew you'd come, I knew you would. Thank God for your Special Forces training." Martina added with a laugh, "But however did you find these other men?"

J.D. and Gabby exchanged a quiet look. "I hired them," he said blandly. "Roberto can reimburse me."

"My poor darling." Martina sighed. "He'll be so frantic."

"How are we going to get out of here?" Gabby asked J.D.

"Wait and see." He glanced toward Apollo. "Ready?" he called.

"Ready!"

"I'm going to draw them out for you. Don't let me down!"

"J.D., no!" Gabby burst out as he leaped out of the brush and started firing toward rustling noises in the undergrowth ahead.

She lost her mind. Afterward it was the only explanation she could come up with. The guerrillas came forward in a rush, and suddenly Gabby was on her feet. She saw a sniper taking dead aim at J.D.; she turned and lifted the heavy weapon and sighted it and pulled the trigger.

It was a miracle that she even hit the guerrilla's shoulder, her aim was so wide. But she did, and with terror she realized that the man had taken aim at her and was about to fire.

"Gabby!" J.D. yelled wildly.

Simultaneously she pulled the trigger again, forgetting to brace the gun in her terror. She was knocked to the ground when she fired. There was a burst of gunfire and, suddenly, a huge, horrible explosion that rocked the ground.

"All right, let's hit it!" First Shirt yelled out.

J.D. dragged Gabby to her feet, and his face showed such terrible fury that she closed her eyes. He didn't even speak. He jerked the gun out of her hands and pushed her ahead of him as he bent to lift Martina to her feet.

"Are you all right, *señorita?*" Laremos asked gently as he joined Gabby.

"My shoulder hurts a little, but I'm...I'm fine," she whispered. She started to turn around, to look behind them, but J.D. was suddenly there.

"Don't look," he said in a tone that dared her to argue. "Get moving."

He was a stranger now, a man she'd never known. His face was like stone, and there was something wild and dangerous in his eyes and in the set of his big body. She didn't say another word. She kept quiet all the long way through the jungle.

"Where are we going?" she finally asked Laremos as they kept moving through the endless jungle.

"In a circle, around my *finca*," he told her. "We have hopes that by now the government troops have rounded up the guerrillas. Apollo has gone in to check."

"So quickly?" she asked, brushing back a strand of matted hair from her sweaty face.

"So quickly," he confirmed. "Your shoulder, it is better?"

"A little bruised, that's all," she said. She felt sick to her stomach. All she wanted was to lie down and forget the past two days altogether.

"I'm so tired," Martina murmured. "Can't we rest?"

"Soon," J.D. said, gently now. "Just a little longer, honey."

"Okay, big brother. I'll trudge along. Gabby, are you holding up okay?"

"Yes, thanks, Martina."

There was a sudden crackling sound and J.D. and the others whirled with their guns leveled as Apollo came leaping through the growth, grinning.

"We're clear!" he shouted. "The government troops just marched the guerrillas away."

"What about the men in the terrorist camp?" Gabby asked.

"They scattered," First Shirt replied. "The guerrillas would have shot them if they'd found them before the government troops showed up. The terrorists have no friends here in Guatemala."

"How sad for them," Martina said, but her eyes flashed. "I do not pity them, not after the ordeal they put me through. Oh, I want my Roberto!"

"We'll send for him the minute we get to my *finca*," Laremos promised her. "The very minute."

Gabby dropped back to put a comforting arm around the smaller, older woman and smiled reassuringly. "It won't be long," she said.

"Absolutely," Laremos agreed. "There. We are home."

The *finca* looked so good that Gabby wanted to kiss it. The outside bore no marks of violence, but inside it was a different story. The furniture was wrecked, the floors scarred. Laremos's dark eyes glittered as he saw the evidence of the brief guerrilla occupation.

"I'm sorry about your house, *señor,*" Martina said gently.

"*Señora,* that you are safe is the most important thing," Laremos said with pride, turning to bow in her direction. "My poor house can be repaired. But your life, once lost, would not have been restored."

"I owe you a great debt," Martina said. Her clothes were torn and her hair hung in wild strands. But she looked spunky for all that. She reached up and kissed Laremos on his tan cheek. *"Muchas gracias."*

Laremos looked embarrassed. "My pleasure, *señora*. I regret that I could not have done more."

"Is everybody all right?" Gabby asked, looking around at the battle-scarred little group with concerned eyes.

"Gabby, you'll spoil us if you worry about us," Apollo said, chuckling.

"Not me." First Shirt glowered at Apollo. "Worry all you want, Gabby. I'll just sit here like a sponge and soak it up."

The others joined in, all except J.D. He kept to himself, looking dangerous and unapproachable until Martina and Gabby left to go up to the room Gabby had shared with him.

"A bath." Martina sighed, taking advantage of the facilities. "I feel so dirty!"

"It must have been horrible," Gabby said, digging out fresh clothes.

"Not as horrible as it could have been. I wasn't abused, at least. That surprised me." She came out of the shower minutes later, toweling her long hair dry. "Your turn. I imagine you feel as mucky as I did."

"Yes, I do." Gabby laughed. "My shoulder hurts and I feel shaky all over."

"You saved J.D.'s life," was Martina's quiet comment. "I can never thank you enough for that. But don't expect him to," she added dryly. "I think his pride's dented. He's very quiet."

"He's been through a lot. They all have. What a great bunch of guys," she said fervently.

"Tell me!" Martina laughed, and despite the weariness in her drawn face, there was joy. "I'd like to kiss every one of them twice. I can't tell you how I felt when I saw J.D. come breaking in that door! Wasn't it lucky that he had that military training?"

Obviously Martina didn't know everything about J.D.'s past, and Gabby wasn't about to betray him. "It sure was," she agreed and disappeared into the bathroom.

Her shoulder was turning blue, but she was grateful to be alive. She still couldn't believe what she'd done. It had been pure instinct when she saw the weapon pointing at J.D. Let him be angry at her—she couldn't be sorry about what she'd done. Even if the man had shot her, it would have been worth it to deflect his aim. If anything had happened to J.D., she might as well have died. She loved him—so much!

The next day, Roberto drove in from the airport and there was a wildly emotional re-union. Gabby, watching, couldn't help the twinge of jealousy she felt. Roberto was crying as he embraced his wife, and un-ashamedly at that. Gabby's eyes darted to J.D., who hadn't said a single word to her since they'd come out of the jungle. They'd all had a good night's sleep, Martina and Gabby sharing the big double bed this time, but his dark mood hadn't lifted. He wouldn't even look at Gabby, and that hurt most of all. She'd only wanted to save him, but it seemed that she'd committed some unforgivable sin.

Chapter Six

Roberto was very Italian, if someone who lived in Sicily could be called Italian, Gabby mused. He was of medium height and thin, with a charm that was immediately apparent when he bent over Gabby's hand.

"It is a pleasure to meet you," he said. He grinned, glancing at J.D., who was talking quietly with Apollo in the living room. "Martina's brother mentions you often."

"Does he?" Gabby asked conversationally, privately wondering whether she even had a job to go back to, now that it was all over. J.D. still hadn't looked in her direction.

"It was bad, Gabby," Martina said from her husband's side, her dark eyes meeting the other girl's green ones warmly. "Jacob and the others...well, it was a miracle that any of us got out. He'll get over it. It has been a long time since he was in the service, you know. It had to affect him."

"Yes, of course," Gabby said, smiling faintly. She couldn't let Martina know the truth. "You look awfully good for somebody who went through what you did."

Martina clung to her husband's arm and smiled. "I have my whole world back again. I feel good. Just a little shaken and homesick." She glanced up at Roberto. "Can we go back today?"

He inclined his head. "As soon as our pilot finishes the meal Laremos was kind enough to provide."

"It will be good to have familiar things around me." Martina sighed. "But I do not think I ever want to go shopping alone again." She shuddered. "From now on, my husband, I will listen when you warn me against such things."

"I had feared that it would happen," Roberto confessed, with a glance at the men scattered around the living room. "Thank God your brother and his friends knew so well what to do. I am sure that the kidnappers would never have let you live." He pulled her into his arms and held her convulsively, his eyes closed, his face contorted. "*Dio,* I could not have lived myself!" he whispered hoarsely.

"Shh," Martina said, comforting him and smiling. She clung to him, and Gabby could only imagine how if felt to be loved so possessively. She experienced a twinge of envy, because nobody had ever cared for her that way. J.D. surely hadn't. He looked as if he were frankly sick of the whole thing, especially Gabby.

"You had better spend a little time with Jacob while you can," Roberto said, releasing Martina. "It may be another year before we see him again." He smiled. "Hopefully, the next time will be under happier circumstances."

"Oh, yes," Martina said wholeheartedly. "Gabby, you must come to Palermo with him next time and visit. Our villa overlooks the sea, and it is so beautiful."

"I'd like that," Gabby said noncommittally. She was thinking that J.D. would probably never take her as far as the corner again, but she didn't say it.

Martina approached her brother, and as J.D. stood up Gabby got a glimpse of his face. It softened magically for his sister. When he smiled at her it was like the sun coming out. Gabby couldn't bear the contrast between the way he'd looked at her in the jungle and the way he looked at his sister. She turned and went toward the bedroom to finish packing.

Later, as she was folding clothes, Martina tapped at the door and entered the room quietly, smiling sheepishly.

"I hate to ask, but do you have some makeup I could borrow?" J.D.'s sister asked. "I feel like a hag."

"Yes, of course, I do," Gabby said quickly, taking her cosmetic case from the dresser. "I didn't bring much, though," she said apologetically as she handed it over, along with a brush. "I kind of figured that we weren't going to be going places that I'd need to dress for."

"Thank you," Martina said and seated herself in front of the mirror. "There!" she exclaimed, smiling ruefully at her face. "Such pleasure, from such a mundane thing," she murmured. "Gabby, there were times when I thought I'd never live long enough to do this again."

"It must have been awful," the taller girl said quietly. "I'm so sorry, Martina."

"My own stupidity," came the reply. "Roberto warned me, but I take after Jacob, I'm afraid. I'm bullheaded and I like my own way." She sat down on the bed and studied Gabby for a long moment. "He will not speak to you, and that hurts, doesn't it?"

Gabby shrugged, taking a long time to fold a T-shirt. "A little."

"If you could only have seen his face in that split second before the recoil threw you to the ground," Martina said solemnly. "It would have been a revelation to you. In all the years of my life, I can only recall once or twice when I've seen that expression in his eyes. Once," she added quietly, "was just after our mother died."

Gabby stared at the pale garment in her hand. "I was so afraid for him," she confided. "I saw that man level his rifle at Jacob, and . . ." She shivered. "It all happened so quickly."

"Yes, I know." Martina stood up. "Gabby, he isn't an easy man. And he's been very restless the past few years. But I think perhaps in you he has found his future. Did you know," she added with a wicked grin, "that you're all I hear about when he calls me these days?"

Gabby laughed nervously, desperate even for crumbs. Her green eyes glowed softly as she looked at Martina. "I'd give anything to be his future," she said quietly. "But he's already said he doesn't want ties or commitment. And I'm dreadfully old-fashioned. Everybody else sleeps around and thinks nothing of it, but I'm just not built for loose affairs."

Martina pursed her lips and then grinned. "Well, well. Poor Jacob."

"Anyway," Gabby said, sighing, "it's probably just a flash in the pan. I've worked for him over two years and he's never looked twice at me until this came up." She glanced at Martina and smiled. "I'm just so glad that you came out of it all right. We were all worried about you, not just J.D."

"Roberto and I must go home today," Martina said. "But you will come and visit us one day. I believe that, even if you don't." Impulsively, she hugged Gabby. "Take care of Jacob for me. He doesn't know that he needs taking care of, so we mustn't let on. But he's so alone, Gabby."

Gabby felt as if she were choking. "Yes," she said. "I know." And it hurt to think just how alone he was, and how much it affected her.

Later, as she wandered around the house restlessly, she met First Shirt coming down the hall, and he stopped to talk to her. "Why the long face, little lady?' he asked with an affectionate smile.

"Work is going to seem like peeling on-ions from now on," she lied, smiling imp-ishly at him.

He laughed heartily. "Now you know why the guys and I don't retire. Hell, I'd rather die on my feet than deteriorate behind a desk." He shrugged. "But it seems to suit Archer."

Her eyes fell. "Yes, I suppose so."

"Hey."

She looked up, and he smiled at her.

"He doesn't like being helped out," he said knowingly. "I ought to know. He threw a punch at me one time when I spotted a guy with a grenade and got to him first. He doesn't like making mistakes. He'll get over what happened out there."

"Will he?" she asked, her eyes wide and sad. "He won't even talk to me."

"Reaction. You have to remember, Gabby, he's been out of action for a while. This sort of thing"—he waved his hand—"you don't forget, but sometimes it brings back bad memories. He got shot up pretty bad once."

"He told me," she said absently.

His eyes narrowed. "Now, that's interesting."

"Just to satisfy my curiosity," she added.

"I used to wonder if he was ever going to settle down," he said enigmatically. "But there was never a special woman."

"I suppose he liked leaving his doors open," she murmured, "in case he couldn't adjust to a desk job."

"Yes, that's what I thought," First Shirt said. His chest rose and fell on a deep breath. "None of us have ties. They're too much of a luxury in this kind of work." He searched her wide eyes. "I'm glad our paths crossed. Take care of Archer. He's gone too far to come back to us, but maybe he doesn't realize it yet."

"I wish you were right, First Shirt," she said with a sad smile.

"My name—my given name—is Matthew."

She smiled. "Matthew."

"Keep in touch once in a while, will you?" he asked as he turned. "Archer's a damned bad correspondent."

"I'll do that," she promised, flattered.

Her eyes followed his lean figure down the hall. She was already thinking about Christmas. Socks, she decided. Lots of socks and gloves. She started back toward the bedroom.

It was deathly quiet after Martina and Roberto left, and one by one the men seemed to vanish. Later she learned that everybody except First Shirt had already left the country for other places, just as secretively as they'd come. She'd grown attached to them in that short space of time. Of course, the circumstances were unusual, to say the least.

Laremos was his charming self at the evening meal, but J.D. was still brooding and he wouldn't look at Gabby.

"When are we going back?" she asked J.D. finally, in desperation.

"Tonight." He bit the words off.

"I'll double-check to make sure I've packed everything." She stood up. "Señor Laremos, thank you for your hospitality. Under different circumstances, it would have been lovely. I'm sorry we didn't get to see the Mayan ruins."

"So am I, Gabby," he said sincerely. "Perhaps you may return someday, and it will be my pleasure to show them to you." He made her a handsome bow and she smiled at him as she left the room.

Minutes later, J.D. joined her, presumably to get his own things packed. He had slept downstairs with the men the night before, but his case was still in the bedroom. Gabby had considered packing for him, but she was nervous about antagonizing him any more.

She looked up from her suitcase when he closed the door. His face was still hard as granite, and his eyes glanced off hers coldly. He didn't say a word as he began to fill the small bag on the chair across from the bed.

"Are you all right?' she asked finally, when the silence became uncomfortable.

"Yes, I'm all right," he said gruffly. "Are you?"

She shrugged and smiled wanly. "It was the experience of a lifetime."

"Wasn't it, though?" he asked curtly. His eyes blazed as he studied her flushed face.

"Why are you so angry?" she asked.

He dropped his eyes to the bag and shoved his combat fatigues into it. "What makes you think I am?"

"You've barely spoken to me since we came back." She moved around the bed to stand beside him, her emotions in turmoil, her mind confused. She looked at his big body and remembered with staggering clarity how it looked without clothing, how it felt to be held by those hard arms and kissed by that mouth.

"Jacob, what have I done?" she asked softly, and touched his arm.

His hard muscles tensed beneath her touch, and when he looked down at her she had to fight the urge to back away.

"What the hell did you think you were playing at out there?" he asked coldly. "Didn't you realize that the bullets weren't blanks, that we weren't acting out some scenario from a television show? You're a dull little secretary, not a professional soldier, and if the force of the recoil hadn't knocked you down, you'd have been killed, you stupid child!"

So that was it. Shirt had been right, his pride was hurt because Gabby had seen a threat and he hadn't. "J.D., if I hadn't shot him, he'd have killed you," she said, trying to reason with him.

He slammed the bag back down. "Am I supposed to thank you?"

Her temper was blazing now too. "Don't strain yourself," she told him icily. "And I am not a dull little secretary!"

"Don't kid yourself," he said, staring at her. "You aren't Calamity Jane and you're never likely to be. You'll get married to some desk jockey and have a dozen kids."

Her face paled and his eyes narrowed when he saw it. "What's wrong, honey?" he taunted. "Were you expecting a proposal from me?"

She turned away. "I expect nothing from you."

"Liar." He caught her arm roughly and swung her around. Seconds later, she was flat on her back on the bed and he was looming over her, holding her down with hands that hurt.

"Jacob, you're bruising me!" she burst out, struggling.

He threw a long, powerful leg across hers and spread-eagled her, his hands on her wrists. "Now fight," he said coldly, "and see how far you get."

She gave up finally and lay breathing heavily, glaring up at him. "What's this supposed to prove, that you're stronger than I am? Okay, I'm not arguing."

His dark eyes wandered slowly over her body, lingering on the curves outlined by her tight jeans and the expanse of bare skin where her sweatshirt had ridden up during the struggle. Her breath caught, because she wasn't wearing a bra, and the hem of the garment was just below the curve of her breasts.

"I wanted you yesterday morning," he said bluntly. "And if you hadn't been a virgin, I'd have taken you. But any woman would have done. You were just a body to me, so if you've been weaving me into your future, forget it."

Her heart leapt in her chest. It was true, she had, but she couldn't let him see just how involved she was emotionally. Very obviously, that wasn't what he wanted from her.

"I haven't asked you for any promises, have I?" she asked quietly, searching his dark eyes. "You're safe, Jacob. I'm not trying to tie you down."

His fingers contracted. "Let's make sure of that, shall we?" he asked in a menacing tone. "Let's make damned sure that you don't ever want to try."

Her lips parted to ask the question, but he moved suddenly. One hand imprisoned both of hers above her head. The other pulled up the sweatshirt, baring her taut breasts to his eyes.

"Now, Gabby, let me show you how a real mercenary treats women."

He did, and she couldn't fight, because he was so much stronger than she was. She lay still, feeling half-afraid of him as he treated her body like a piece of used merchandise. He shamed her, humiliated her, covering her with his own taut body, while his hands touched and gripped and his body moved suggestively, making a travesty of everything she felt for him.

"Do you like it?" he growled against her bruised mouth as his hands moved lower on her pinned body and contracted, grinding her hips against his. "Because this is how it would be if I took you. Quick and rough and purely for my own pleasure. And if you're remembering yesterday morning, don't," he added. "Because that was a flash in the pan. This is the reality. This, and this . . . !"

He hurt her, and the crush of his mouth was as suggestive as the motion of his hard body. She tried to struggle away from him, but that only made it worse. He forced her arms down into the mattress and his body overwhelmed hers in an intimacy that made her gasp.

He laughed coldly. "Are you shocked? You wanted it yesterday. Come on, honey. I won't let you get pregnant. How about it?" And he kissed her again, cruelly, oblivious to the tears of shame and humiliation running hotly down her cheeks as he whispered graphic, crude remarks before his mouth forced hers open and penetrated it.

When he finally tired of the game and rolled away, she couldn't even move. She lay there, bruised and emotionally devastated, her face pale, her eyes closed. Tears ran in a flood down her cheeks and her body shook with sobs.

"Damn you, J.D.," she wept, flushed with fury. "Damn you!"

"That's how I am with a woman," he said coldly, ignoring the trembling of her body, the terrible hurt in her eyes. "That's how it would have been yesterday if I'd had the time and I could have coaxed you into it. Your body arouses me and I want it. But anything would have done. I just needed to forget what was ahead, the same way I've forgotten it a hundred times before with a hundred other women." His voice was bitter and he turned away. "So set your sights on some other man, and don't weave romantic daydreams around me. I've just shown you the reality. Remember it."

She didn't move. She couldn't. She was trembling too much, and she felt sick and empty. Her eyes looked up into his, bright with furious anger. Something of her pain and shame must have shown in them, because he turned away and, grabbing up his suitcase, went to the door without another glance.

"Bring your bag and let's go," he said in a harsh tone.

She watched him close the door and then she managed to get to her feet. His taunting voice would haunt her as long as she lived. She would resign, of course, but she didn't know how she was going to manage to look at him while she worked out a two-week notice. Maybe he'd let her go immediately. The only problem was that she didn't have another job to go to. Her rent and car payments wouldn't wait while she went without work.

Minutes later, wearing a fresh green pullover blouse with a matching sweater and the same jeans, and with her hair carefully pulled back in a bun, she left the bedroom, her suitcase in hand. She was still pale, but makeup had camouflaged the rest of what J.D. had done to her.

He didn't even glance in her direction as she came back into the living room. Apparently, he'd shut her out of his mind already, and she wished she had the ability to do the same with him. The scars his brutality had left on her emotions would be a long time healing. She'd loved him. How could he hurt her that way? How could he?

She tried to disguise her anguish and hoped that she succeeded. She said goodbye to Laremos and got into the station wagon with First Shirt while J.D. said his own farewells.

Shirt gave her a brief but thorough scrutiny and laid one lean, wiry hand over the steering wheel. "What did he do to you?" he asked.

She lifted a startled face. "Why... nothing."

"Don't lie," he said gently. "I've known him a long time. Are you okay?"

She shifted restlessly in the seat, refusing to let her eyes go past Shirt to J.D., who was standing apart with Laremos. "Yes, I'm okay," she said. "Of course, I'll be a lot better once I get out of his life."

"Whew." He whistled ruefully. "That bad?"

"That bad." She gripped her purse tightly in her lap.

"Gabby," he said gently, with a tiny smile, "have you ever known a fighting fish to lie down when he hit the bait? Don't expect to draw him in without a little effort."

She glared at him. "I'd like to put a hook in him, but not to land him."

"Give it a little time," he said. "He's been alone most of his life. It's new to him, needing someone."

"He doesn't need me," she said shortly.

"I'm not convinced of that," he replied. He studied her affectionately. "I think he's met his match. You're a pretty damned good shot for a lady who's never used an automatic weapon before. Laremos said you learned fast."

She pursed her lips, studying her purse. "It wasn't a hard weapon to learn," she told him. "There were only three positions to remember with the change lever—top for safety, middle for bursts and bottom for single shots. And actually, I have shot a .22-caliber rifle before. Mama and I used to hunt rabbits. But it didn't have a kick like that AK-47.''

He smiled as she rubbed her shoulder. ''I don't imagine so. Is your mother still alive?''

She nodded, smiling back. ''She lives in Lytle, Texas. There's a small ranch, and she has a few head of cattle. It's not nearly as big as the one she and Daddy had, but when he died, she decided to retire. Sort of.''

''And she hunts?'' he asked.

''Hunts, rides, ropes, and can outcuss most veteran cowboys,'' she told him. ''She's quite a character.''

''You're a character yourself,'' he said. ''When J.D. told me he took you along on secret meetings, I began to realize that he had an unusual relationship with you. J.D. doesn't trust anybody except his sister and me.''

That wasn't bragging, either, she realized. Just a statement of fact. ''He doesn't trust Laremos.''

''Neither do I,'' he whispered, smiling.

She burst out laughing, but the amusement faded immediately as J.D. started toward the car, and she felt herself freezing up.

But she needn't have worried. J.D. climbed into the back seat and slammed the door, waving to Laremos.

"Be back in a few hours, Boss," Shirt called to him. Laremos grinned and waved, and they were under way.

It was a long trip to the airport, not because of distance but because of the tension between Gabby and J.D. Despite First Shirt's efforts to keep things casual, Gabby drew into herself and didn't say a word all the way.

It was like that during the flight back as well. Gabby was relieved to find that their seats were not together. She was sandwiched between a businessman and a young girl. J.D.'s seat was farther back. Not one word had passed between them when they landed at O'Hare airport in the wee hours of the morning.

It took her a long time to find a place in the swollen ranks of departing passengers. She didn't look back to see where J.D. was either. Her only thought was to get back to her apartment. After that she'd face the thought of leaving J.D. forever, of finding another job and getting on with her life.

At last she reached the front of the terminal and stepped out into the breezy night air that carried the sound of distant car horns and city smells that had become so familiar. There was no cab in sight, but Gabby wasn't daunted. She'd just call one.

"Come on," J.D. said tersely, appearing just behind her. "I'll drive you."

She glared at him. "I'd rather be mugged."

"You might be, at this hour, alone," he said matter-of-factly. "What's the matter, afraid of me?" he taunted.

She was; he'd made her afraid. But she was too proud to let him see how much.

After a minute, she turned and followed him toward the parking lot. A little later, they were winding their way back into Chicago.

"Have you decided what you're going to do?" he asked.

She knew instinctively what he meant. "Yes. I'm going to try to find a job in the computer field. I like working with them."

He glanced toward her. "I thought you enjoyed legal work. It's too bad, to let that paralegal training go to waste."

"I'm tired of legal work," she said non-committally. What she meant was that she couldn't take the risk of running into J.D. accidentally after she'd quit. It would be too painful.

He shrugged and calmly lit a cigarette as he drove. "It's your life. You'd better call that agency Monday morning and have them send over some applicants. I'll let Dick do the interviewing this time," he added with a cold laugh.

Her fingers clenched on her purse. She stared out of the window at the river.

"No comment?" he prodded.

"About what?" she asked indifferently.

He sighed heavily and took another draw from the cigarette. One more turn and he pulled the car into a parking spot in front of her apartment building.

She got out and waited for him to get her carry-on bag. "Don't bother walking me up," she said.

He glared down at her. "I wasn't aware that I'd offered."

Her anger exploded. "I hate you," she said in a venomous whisper.

"Yes, I know you do," he said with a cold smile.

She whirled on her heel and started toward the door of the building.

"Gabby," he called curtly.

She stopped with her hand on the door, but didn't turn. "What?"

"You'll work a two-week notice. Every day of it. Or I'll make sure you don't work again. Clear?"

She'd been thinking about not showing up at all on Monday. But when she turned and saw his eyes, she realized, not for the first time, what a formidable adversary he made. She hated to give in, but the necessity of finding a new job made her do so gracefully.

"Why, Mr. Brettman, I wouldn't miss a minute of it," she said with sweet mockery. "See you Monday."

Chapter Seven

The last thing she felt like doing Monday morning was going into the office. To make things worse, her shoulder was aching like mad. But that didn't stop Gabby. She put on a beige suit with a jazzy, multicolored blouse, pinned up her hair, and went to work. Might as well get it over with, she told herself. She'd go back to the office, work out her notice, and get another job. Sure. Simple.

Explaining that to her mother back home in Lytle, Texas, had not been quite so simple.

"But I thought you loved your job!" her mother had gasped. "Why are you quitting? Listen, Gabby, what's happened?"

"Nothing, Mama," she'd said quickly. "It's just that Mr. Brettman may not be in Chicago much longer." She lied on impulse. "You see, he has prospects in another area, and I don't really want to relocate."

"Where would he go?"

"Now, Mama," she said, "you know I don't like to pry into Mr. Brettman's business."

"That Mr. Dice, his partner, why couldn't you still work for him?" her mother demanded gruffly. "Better yet, why don't you come home and get married?"

Gabby chewed on her lip so that she wouldn't say anything hasty. She had visions of her mother providing a groom, a minister, and a loaded gun for motivation. It made her want to giggle, which would have infuriated her mother.

"Gabby, you aren't in trouble?" her mother had added in a strange tone.

"No, Mama, I'm not in trouble. Now don't get upset. It may all fall through anyway."

"I like Mr. Brettman," her mother said roughly. "That one time I met him when I visited you, he seemed like a nice man to me. Why does he want to move anyway? He isn't getting married?"

"J.D.? Get married?" Gabby laughed mirthlessly. "That would make the world record books."

"He'll have to get married someday," came the curt reply.

"Think so?" Already Gabby could picture him in fatigues rushing some stronghold with Shirt and Apollo. But she couldn't tell her mother that!

"Of course. It happens to everybody. He'll get tired of living alone someday. Your father did. That's when I nabbed him." Gabby could almost see her grin.

"Are you tired of living alone?" Gabby asked suddenly. It had been ten years since her father's death. Yet her mother didn't even date.

"I don't live alone, baby. I live with my memories. I had the best man God ever made. I don't want second best."

"You're just fussy," Gabby said accusingly.

"Yes, I am. You be fussy too. Honey, think about coming home. That Chicago place is pretty big, and if Mr. Brettman isn't going to be around, I'd worry about you."

"I'll think about it," Gabby promised.

She hated thinking about it. It made her face the fact that she wouldn't be seeing J.D. again. Whether or not he went back to the old life, he'd made it impossible for her to work for him anymore. He'd forced her into resigning, whether consciously or unconsciously. And now here she was losing her boss, her job, and her heart all in the space of three days. So little time to change so much of her future. It might have been better if she'd stayed behind and never known the truth about J.D.

When she got to the office, it was clear that J.D. had not yet come in. Richard Dice was sitting on her desk with his arms folded across his chest, looking murderous.

"Morning, Dick," she said with a forced smile.

"Thank God you're back." He sighed. "That temporary girl didn't work out, and the agency hasn't called me about a replacement. Where's J.D.?"

"Don't ask me," she replied, calmly shedding her jacket and putting her purse in the desk drawer. She tucked her glasses on top of her head while she searched through the calendar for appointments that had been made by both the temporary girl and herself.

"Didn't he come back?" Dick persisted.

"Yes." She stared at him. "You mean he hasn't been in touch with you?"

"Not yet. Well?" he burst out. "What happened? How's Martina? Did they pay the ransom?"

"You're chock-full of questions." She sighed in turn. "Yes, Martina's safe. No, they didn't have to pay the ransom. And anything else you want to know, ask J.D., because I don't want to talk about it."

Dick looked at the ceiling. "You disappear for days, and all I get is one long-winded sentence?"

"You should have come with us," she said conversationally. "Then you wouldn't have to take up my time asking questions. Did you take care of Mrs. Turnbull's divorce yesterday?"

"Yes," he murmured absently. "Judge Amherst called. He wants to discuss the Landers case with J.D. before he makes a decision about the trial date."

Gabby made a note of it.

Dick was studying her closely. "You look bad."

She smiled. "Thank you. What a lovely thing to be told."

He flushed. "I mean, you look worn out."

"You try crawling through a jungle on your belly with an AK-47 and see how you look," she replied.

"Jungle? On your belly? What's an AK-47?"

She got up from her desk and started filing some folders that Dick had left there. "Ask J.D."

"But he isn't here!"

She glowered at the file folders. "Maybe he's out buying a new crossbow," she muttered.

"A what?" But she didn't hear him. He grumbled something and walked into his office, slamming the door behind him. She glanced over her shoulder. "Well, somebody's in a snit," she said to the filing cabinet.

It was a good two hours before J.D. came in, looking as neat as a pin in his vested gray suit.

"Any messages?" he asked Gabby, just as he used to.

"No, sir," she replied, and she sounded the same too, except that she wouldn't meet his eyes. "Dick took care of the Turnbull case for you, and Judge Amherst wants you to call him."

He nodded. "What have I got on the calendar for this afternoon?"

"Mr. Parker is coming by at one to get you to draw up that incorporation for him, and you have three other appointments after him."

He turned toward his office. "Get your pen and pad and let's get the correspondence out of the way."

"Yes, sir."

"Oh, there you are, J.D.," Richard called from the doorway of his own office. "Welcome back. Would you tell me what happened? Gabby's got a case of the clams."

"So have I," J.D. informed him. "Everything's okay. Martina and Roberto are back in Palermo by now, and the kidnappers were taken care of. How about lunch?"

"Sorry," Richard said, smiling. "I've got a luncheon appointment with a client. Rain check?"

"Sure."

Gabby followed J.D. into the office and left the door open. If he noticed, or cared, he didn't let on. He eased his formidable frame into the big swivel chair behind the desk and picked up a handful of letters.

He started dictating and she kept her eyes on her pad until he finished. Her fingers ached and so did her back from sitting so straight, but she didn't move an inch until he dismissed her.

"Gabby," he called as she started toward the door.

"Yes, sir?"

He fingered a pencil on his desk, and his dark eyes stared at it. "How's your shoulder?" he asked.

She shrugged. "It's still a little sore, but I can't complain." She clasped the pad tightly against her breasts. She studied his impassive face quietly. "By the way, do you need written notice, or is a verbal one satisfactory?"

His eyes came up. "Wait," he said quietly.

"I have to get another job. I can't do that if I'm obligated to you for more than two weeks," she said with remarkable calm.

His jaw clenched. "You don't have to quit."

"Like hell I don't!" she returned.

"Things will get back to normal!" he roared. "Is it too much to ask you to give it a chance? We got along well enough before!"

"Yes, we did, before you treated me like a streetwalker!" she burst out.

He saw the hatred in her eyes, in her rigid posture. His gaze fell to the pencil again. "You won't be easy to replace," he said in an odd tone.

"Sure I will," she said venomously. "All you have to do is call the agency and ask for somebody stupid and naïve who won't get too close and loves being shot at!"

His face paled. "Gabby..."

"What's going on?" Richard asked from the open door. He looked aghast. He'd never heard Gabby raise her voice in the two years he'd known her, and here she stood yelling at J.D. at the top of her lungs.

"None of your business," they chimed in together, glaring at him.

He hunched his thin shoulders and grinned sheepishly. "Excuse me, I feel a sudden urge to eat lunch. Goodbye!"

They didn't even notice his leaving. J.D. glared at Gabby, and she glared back.

"I'm too set in my ways to break in somebody new," he said finally. "And you'd be bored to death working for anybody else and you know it."

"It's my life," she reminded him.

He got up from the desk and she backed away, her eyes wide and angry and afraid. The fear was what stopped him in his tracks.

"I wasn't going to make a grab for you, Miss Darwin."

"Shall I drop to my knees and give thanks?" she asked, glaring back. "You'll never make the list of the ten top lovers, that's for sure."

"No, I don't imagine so," he said quietly. "But I didn't realize how much I'd frightened you." He studied her closely. "Gabby, I never meant to go that far."

"I wasn't going to try to drag you in front of a minister," she said, lowering her voice. "I was curious about you, just as you were curious about me. It's over now. I don't want ties either."

"Don't leave," he said quietly. "I'll never touch you again."

"That isn't the point," she told him, shifting restlessly from one foot to the other. "I...I don't want to work for you anymore."

His dark eyes searched hers slowly, quietly. "Why?"

That was rich. Was she going to tell him that her heart would break if she had to work with him day in and day out, loving him hopelessly, eating her heart out for him? That was what would happen too. She'd go on mooning over him and never be able to date anybody else. Worse, she'd sit cringing as the days went by, wondering when he would throw it all in and rush back to First Shirt and Apollo. Now that he'd gotten a taste of the old, free life again, she had to expect that it would happen.

"There's no job security here," she said finally, putting her nameless fears into mundane words that couldn't possibly express her real feelings.

He drew a cigarette from his pocket and lit it, staring at her through the smoke. "You're guessing that I'll go back to the old life?'' he asked coldly.

She shook her head. "No, J.D.—anticipating. Shirt said that you had the bug again,'' she confided. "I want a dull, routine employer who won't go rushing off to save the world at a minute's notice."

His jaw tightened. "It's my life. How I live it is my business."

"But of course," she said with a sickeningly sweet smile. "That's exactly what I meant. Out of sight, out of mind."

That made him angry. His dark eyes glittered as he scowled at her. "After what we shared in that room at Laremos's house?'' he asked bluntly.

Her eyes narrowed. "Perhaps we're thinking of different things,'' she retorted. "I have a very vivid memory of being treated like the worst kind of Saturday-night pickup!"

He turned away and went to the window, his back rigid. "There were reasons."

"Of course there were!'' she shot back. "You wanted to make sure that I didn't get any ideas about you just because you made a pass at me. Okay! I got the message and I'm going, just as fast as I can!" she said. "Do you really think I could forget what happened in Guatemala and go on working for you?"

He studied the cigarette in his fingers. "Maybe I'll settle down," he said after a minute.

"Maybe you will, but what concern is that of mine?" she asked. "You're my employer, not my lover."

He turned just as the phone on her desk rang. She rushed to answer it, grateful for the diversion. Fortunately, it was an angry, long-winded client. She smiled wickedly as she transferred the call to J.D.'s phone. While he was talking, she escaped to lunch, leaving him listening helplessly to the venomous divorcée on the other end of the line.

But once she was out of the office and eating a hamburger at a local fast-food restaurant, the smile vanished and gloom set in. She'd read about men who couldn't marry, who were too freedom-loving for marriage. But until J.D. came along, she hadn't known what anguish there could be in loving someone like that. Now she did, and her nights would be plagued with nightmares about hearing someday he'd died in combat. Or worse, that he was serving time in some filthy foreign jail for interfering in the internal politics of another nation.

If Martina had known the truth, maybe she could have helped talk some sense into him. But Gabby hadn't dared to tell her. J.D. would never forgive Gabby if she did.

An hour later, she dragged herself back into the office, only to find J.D. gone. There was a terse note on her desk, informing her that he'd gone to meet a client and that she was to cancel his appointments; he wouldn't be in until the next day.

She picked up the phone and started dialing. Was he really seeing a client? The thought tormented her, even after she left the office. Perhaps he'd already packed his bag and gone off in search of the sun. She cried herself to sleep, hating herself for worrying. If this was any indication of the future, she'd do well to hurry about finding another job.

The next day she forced herself to search the want ads for positions in between answering the phone, using the copier, and running the computer. J.D. still hadn't come in, and she was grateful for Dick's dictation and the hectic rush of the office. It kept her from thinking about J.D.

When he walked in the door just before lunch, it was all she could do not to jump up and throw herself into his arms. But she remembered that he didn't want ties so she forced herself to greet him calmly and hand him his messages.

"Worried about me?" he asked with apparent carelessness, but his eyes were watchful.

She looked up with hard-won composure, her eyebrows arched behind her reading glasses. "Worried? Why?"

He drew in a slow breath and turned on his heel to walk into his office. He slammed the door behind him.

She stuck out her tongue at it and picked up her purse. "Going to lunch," she said into the intercom and started out the door.

"Gabby."

She turned. He was standing in his office doorway, looking lonely and hesitant.

"Have lunch with me," he said.

She held up the newspaper. "Sorry. I'm going interviewing."

His face hardened, his eyes narrowed. "Don't."

Her soft heart almost melted under that half pleading stare. But she couldn't give in, not now. In the long run, it would be easier to eat her heart out from a safe distance. She'd die working with him, knowing that all he was capable of giving her was lust or a business relationship.

"I have to," she said quietly. "It's for the best."

"For whom?" he demanded.

"For both of us!" she burst out. "I can't bear to be in the same office with you!"

Something indescribable happened to his face. And because it hurt to see him that way, she turned and all but ran out the door. It didn't occur to her until much later how he might have taken her remark. She'd meant she couldn't bear to be with him because she loved him so, but he probably thought it was because of his brutal treatment of her at the *finca*. Well, he had been brutal. But he'd apologized, and some part of her understood why he'd acted that way. He was just trying to open her eyes to the futility of loving him. To spare her more hurt. Anyway, she told herself, her remark wouldn't faze him. He didn't care about her, so how in the world could she hurt him?

She applied for two jobs in offices a few blocks away. In one job she would be operating a computer. She knew how to do that, so it would be easy. The other was to work as a secretary for an international firm.

When she went back to the office, J.D. was gone again. Just as well, she thought. She had to get used to not seeing him. The thought was excruciatingly painful, but she was realistic enough to know that the pain would pass one day. After all, as J.D. himself had said, there was no future for her with him. He'd gone to elaborate lengths to make sure she knew that. And since she couldn't spend the day crying, she forced herself to keep her mind strictly on the job.

Chapter Eight

J.D. was so reserved after that day that he barely spoke to Gabby at all, except when absolutely necessary for business. And all the time he scowled and snapped, like a wounded animal.

"Have you heard anything about your job interviews yet?" he asked Friday morning, glaring at her over a piece of correspondence to which he had just dictated an answer.

"I hope to hear Monday about the computer job," she said quietly. "The other one didn't work out."

He pursed his lips thoughtfully. "So it may not be all that easy to find something else," he commented.

She met his level stare. "If nothing works out in Chicago, I'm going home."

He didn't move. He studied her intently. "To Texas."

She lowered her gaze to her steno pad. "That's right."

"What would you do in Texas?"

"I'd help Mama."

He put down the letter. " 'Help Mama,' " he scoffed, glaring at her. "Your mother would drive you to drink in less than a week, and you know it."

"How dare you . . . !" she began hotly.

"Gabby, your mother is a sweet lady," he said, "but her life-style and yours are worlds apart. You'd fight all the time, or you'd find yourself being led around like a lamb."

Her breasts rose and fell softly. "Yes, I know," she said after a minute. "But it's better than the unemployment line, isn't it?"

"Stay with me," he said. "I think, if you'll just give it time, it will work out.

Can't you forget how I treated you that one time?''

"Don't make it harder for me," she said.

"Is it hard, to walk out that door and never seen me again?" he asked bluntly.

Her chin trembled just a little. "You've got nothing to give—you told me so. You've left me no choice but to leave."

"Yes, that was what I said," he agreed. "I went to impossible lengths to show you just how uncommitted I was, to make sure that you didn't try to cling too closely." He sighed heavily and his hands moved restlessly on the desk. "And now I can't look myself in the mirror, thinking about the way you cringe every time I come near you." He got up from the desk and stared out of the window, stretching as if he were stiff all over. "I've never needed anyone," he said after a minute, without turning. "Not even when I was a boy. I was always looking out for Martina and Mama. There was never anyone who gave a damn about me except them. I've been alone all my life. I've wanted it that way."

"I've told you until I'm blue in the face, I'm not trying to trap you!"

He lifted his head and looked at her. "Yes, I realize that now. I want you to try to understand something," he said after a minute. "I spent a lot of my life in the military. I got used to a certain way of doing things, a certain way of life. I thought it had stopped being important to me. And then Martina was kidnapped."

"And you got a taste of it again," she said quietly, searching his face. "And now you're not sure you can be just a lawyer for the rest of your life."

"You read me very well."

"We've worked together for a long time." She stared down at the steno pad and pen in her hands, glad that he couldn't see her heart breaking. "I'll miss you from time to time, J.D. Whatever else this job was, it was never dull."

"If you stay," he said quietly, "I might be able to stay too."

"What do I have to do with it?" she asked with a nervous laugh. "My goodness, the world is full of competent paralegals. You might like your next one a lot better than you like me. I have a nasty temper and I talk back, remember?''

"I remember so much about you," he said surprisingly. "When I started trying to tear you out of my life, I discovered just how deep the taproot went. You've become a habit with me, Gabby, like early morning coffee and my newspaper. I can't get up in the morning without thinking about coming to work and finding you here.''

"You'll find new habits," she said. Was that all she was, a habit?

"I'm trying to make you understand that I don't want to acquire any new habits," he growled. "I like things the way they are, I like the routine of them.''

"No, you don't," she told him, glaring. "You just said so. You want to go back to all the uncertainties of being a mercenary, and risking your life day after day. You want to go adventuring.''

"You make it sound like a disease," he said shortly.

"Isn't it? You're afraid to feel anything. Shirt, Apollo, Semson, all of them are men who've lost something they can't live without. So they're looking for an end, not a beginning. They don't have anything to lose, and nothing to go back to. I learned so much in those three days, J.D. I learned most of all that I have everything to live for. I don't want that kind of freedom."

"You've never had it," he reminded her.

"That's true," she agreed. "But you've spent five years working to build a life for yourself, and you've made a huge success of it. Several people owe their lives, and their freedom, to you. Are you really crazy enough to throw all that away on a pipe dream?"

"Freedom isn't always won in a court of law," he growled.

"How then—with an Uzi and a few blocks of C-4?" she asked. "There are other ways to promote change than with bombs and bullets!"

He drew in a short breath. "You don't understand."

"That's right, I don't. And for your information, I've lost all my illusions about the exciting life of a soldier of fortune." She stood up with her pad in hand. "I'll go and transcribe this."

He watched her walk to the door. "Wait a minute," he said.

She paused with her hand on the door-knob and watched him come around the desk. She felt a twinge of fear as he came close to her. He towered over her, his blue pin-striped suit emphasizing the strength of his muscular body.

She opened the door and moved through it, trying not to show fear, but he saw right through her.

"No," he said softly, shaking his head. "No, don't run. I won't hurt you."

"You used to say that a lot, and I listened one time too many," she said with a nervous laugh. She backed up until she got the width of her desk between them. "I have to get these typed," she added, lifting the steno pad.

His dark eyes had an oddly bleak look in them. "It's real, isn't it, that fear?" he asked.

She sat down in her chair, avoiding his piercing gaze. "I have work to do, J.D."

He propped himself on the corner of the desk with a graceful, fluid movement.

"Don't panic," he said quietly. "I'm not coming any closer than this."

She stiffened. She couldn't help it.

"I should never have hurt you that way," he said, staring down at her clenched fingers. "I overreacted. Someday I'll try to explain it to you."

"There won't be any 'someday,'" she said tersely. "You'll be off blowing things up and I'll be programming computers."

"Will you stop that?" he growled. He fumbled for a cigarette.

"Would you mind waiting until I cover my diskettes?" she asked coldly, reaching to pull them out of the double-disk-drive computer. "Smoke and dust can cause them to crash."

He waited impatiently until she'd replaced the diskettes in their envelopes and stored them in their box before he lit the cigarette.

She glared at him. "I can't transcribe your letters until I can use the computer," she said matter-of-factly.

"So the letters can wait," he said. "Gabby, I swear to God I didn't mean to frighten you that much. I was shaken by what we'd been through, I was half-crazy..." He ran a hand through his hair. "I forgot how innocent you were too. I want you to know that under ordinary circumstances it wouldn't be like that for you with a man."

"With another man, perhaps not." She bit off the words.

"Gabby, what happened the morning before the mission didn't frighten you."

She felt herself go hot all over at the reminder, at the memories that flooded her mind. She remembered the touch of his hard mouth, the feel of his body, the tenderness of the fingers that searched over her soft, aching flesh....

"You were a different man then," she shot back. "You wouldn't even speak to me when we got back to the *finca,* you wouldn't look at me. You acted like a stranger, and then you attacked me!"

He stared down at the cigarette in his hand. "Yes, I know. I've hardly slept since."

His chest rose and fell slowly. He leaned over to crush out his cigarette in the spotless ashtray on her desk. He was so close, she could see the harsh shadows under his eyes.

"Would you consider having supper with me?" he asked.

Her heart jumped, but she didn't take time to decide whether it was from anticipation or fear. "No," she said bluntly, before she had time to change her mind.

He sighed. "No." His broad, hard mouth twisted into a rueful smile. He let his eyes wander slowly over her face. "Somehow, storming that terrorist camp seems like kid stuff compared to getting past your defenses, Gabby."

"Why bother?" she asked quietly. "I'll be here only another week."

The light went out of his eyes. He got to his feet and turned back toward his office. He paused at the doorway with his broad back to her. He seemed about to say something, about to turn. Then he straightened, went on into his office, and closed the door quietly behind him. Gabby hesitated just for a minute; then she booted up the computer again and concentrated on typing the business letters he'd dictated.

Saturday morning arrived sunny and with the promise of budding flowers. Gabby hated the city on such delightfully spring-like days. She was brooding in her apartment, in the midst of doing her laundry, when a knock sounded at the door.

She couldn't imagine who might be visiting, unless her mother had gotten worried and had come all the way from Lytle to see her. That thought bothered her, and she went rushing to open the door.

J.D. lifted a heavy eyebrow. "Were you expecting me?" he asked with a faint grin.

She faltered, trying to think of a graceful way to ask him to leave. While she was debating, he walked into the apartment and sat down on her sofa.

"I thought you might like to have lunch with me," he said out of the blue, studying her slender figure in faded jeans and a striped pullover knit shirt.

She realized as she stared down at him that he looked different, and then she noticed what he was wearing. She'd never seen J.D.

in anything but neat suits or jungle fatigues. But now he was wearing blue jeans as worn and faded as her own, with a western-style blue chambray shirt and boots. She stood there staring at him because she couldn't help it. He was so devastatingly handsome and masculine that he made her feel weak-kneed—from a distance, at least. She was still a little uneasy being alone with him.

"I won't pounce," he said softly. "I won't make a single move that you don't want. I won't even touch you, if that's what it takes. Spend the day with me, though, Gabby."

"Why should I?" she asked curtly.

He smiled wistfully. "Because I'm lonely."

Something in the region of her heart gave way. It must have been her soft brain, she told herself, because there was no logic in giving in to him. It would only make it harder to leave. And she had to leave. She couldn't bear staying around him, feeling the way she felt.

"You've got friends," she said evasively.

"Sure," he said, standing. He stuck his hands in his pockets, stretching the jeans flat across his muscular stomach and powerful thighs. "Sure, I've got friends. There's Shirt, and Apollo..."

"I mean...friends here in the city," she said hesitantly.

He was silent for a moment. "I've got you. No one else."

She gave in. Without another argument. How did you fight a flat statement like that, especially when you knew it was true? He'd said himself that he trusted no one except her. Friendship naturally involved trust.

"Okay," she said after a minute. "But just lunch."

"Just lunch," he agreed. And he didn't come close to her, or pressure her, or do anything to make her wary of him. He waited patiently while she closed the apartment door and locked it, and he walked beside her like a graceful giant as they left the building and got into his car.

Chapter Nine

It was an odd kind of day for Gabby. She thought she knew every one of J.D.'s moods, but that day he was different, in a way that she couldn't quite define.

He strolled beside her through the trees in the nearby park, then along the beach that edged the lake, watching birds rise and soar, watching boats sail and putter by. The wind tossed his dark hair and the sun made it glint blue-black. And Gabby thought she'd never felt like this in her life, free and yet protected and wildly excited, all at the same time. It was hard to remember that this was more of an end than a beginning. J.D. had a guilty conscience about the way he'd treated her and was trying to make amends before she left. That was all. She had to stop trying to make more out of it.

His fingers brushed hers as they walked, and he glanced down, watching her carefully.

"Looking for warts?" she asked, attempting to lessen the tension between them.

"Not really," he murmured. "I'm trying to decide what you'd do if I made a grab for your hand."

That irrepressible honesty again. She smiled and gave him her slender fingers, feeling trembly as he slowly locked them into his own. She was remembering that flight to Mexico and how he'd caressed her fingers with his own, and the remark he'd made about bodies fitting together that way. Her face burned.

He chuckled softly. "I wonder if you could possibly be thinking about the same thing I am, Gabby?" he murmured.

"I wish you'd mind your own business," she told him.

"I'm trying, but you're pretty transparent, honey. You still blush delightfully."

She tugged her fingers away and, to her disappointment, he let them go.

"No pressure," he said when she gave him a puzzled glance. "None at all. I'll take only what you give me."

She stopped, facing him. Nearby, the lake lapped softly at the shore and some children made wild sounds down the beach as they chased each other.

"What are you trying to do?" she asked.

He sighed. "Show you that I'm not a monster," he said.

"I never thought you were," she replied.

"Then why does this happen every time I come close to you?" he asked. His big hands shot out and caught her by the waist, dragging her against him.

She panicked. Her body twisted violently, her hands fought him. It was all over in seconds, but his face had gone white, and her own was flushed with exertion and anger.

She drew her lower lip between her teeth and bit it. J.D. looked . . . odd.

He gave a hard laugh and turned away. With unsteady fingers, he managed to light a cigarette despite the breeze. He took a long, steadying draw from it.

"Oh, God." He laughed bitterly. "I did a job on you, didn't I?"

Her legs were none too steady, but she managed to calm her voice enough to trust it with speech. "I'd never been handled roughly by a man before, J.D.," she told him. "And you said some pretty harsh things."

He turned, staring down at her. "Some pretty explicit ones." His dark eyes wandered slowly down her body, lingering on the soft curves as he lifted the cigarette to his mouth. "By the time I got around to that, I'd long forgotten my motives."

She blinked. "I don't understand."

His eyes found the horizon across the lake, and he smoked his cigarette quietly. "It doesn't matter," he said vaguely. He finished the cigarette and ground it out under his boot.

"You've gone back to smoking all the time," she said.

His shoulders rose and fell. "There doesn't seem much point in quitting now."

She wrapped her arms tightly across her breasts as she watched him walk down the beach. She followed him, searching for words.

"If you hadn't grabbed me like that, I wouldn't have fought you," she said curtly. She hadn't wanted to tell him that, but he looked as if her reaction to him had devastated him. Her marshmallow heart was going to do her in, she told herself when he stopped in his tracks and gaped at her.

"What?" he burst out.

She turned away, letting the wind blow her long, dark hair around. She couldn't manage another word.

He moved closer, but slowly this time. His hands came up to her face, hesitantly cupping it. Her heart pounded, but she didn't pull away.

His chiseled mouth parted as he looked deeply into her eyes. His face was rigid with control. She could feel the warm threat of his body against her, smell the musky scent of his cologne.

"Half of what I told you in that room was true," he said in a husky whisper. "In my younger days, I never gave a damn about the woman I took. But now, it matters. What I did to you, the things I said... I can't sleep, I can't eat. It haunts me."

"Why?" She, too, whispered.

His thumbs edged toward her mouth. "I... cared."

Her pupils dilated, darkening the green of her eyes. "Cared?"

He bent, and his hands were unsteady as they cupped her face. "I kept thinking about how close I came to losing you out there in the jungle," he whispered against her lips. "I wanted to purge myself of the memory and the emotion. So I hurt you." His face hardened, his heavy brows drew together. "But what I did to you... hurt me more." His hard lips brushed hers, nibbled at them. "You've seen me at my worst. Trust me now, Gabby. Let me show you... how tender I can be."

She wanted it almost frantically. She wanted a memory to take down the long, lonely years with her. So she let him have her mouth, as he wanted it. And his lips taught hers new sensations, new ways of touching and exploring.

He moaned softly, and his hands contracted, but his mouth was still tender even though she could feel his big body going rigid against her.

Her eyes opened and found his watching her, passion blazing out of them, a hunger like nothing she'd ever seen in him.

He lifted his head, his breath unsteady on her moist, parted lips. "Don't go cold on me," he whispered. "Not yet."

She swallowed, and her breasts lifted and fell with her breath. "Jacob..."

His eyes closed as though he were in pain. "I thought I'd never hear you say my name like that again," he said harshly.

Her hands were against the front of his shirt, and she didn't even know how they'd landed there. She was all too aware of what was under it, of how it felt to bury her fingers in that thick, cool mat of curling hair.

"Don't make it difficult for me," she whispered helplessly.

His hands slid around to the back of her head, tilting her face upward. "Do you think it's easy for me, letting you go?"

"Yes," she said with a trembling smile. "You said yourself that you didn't want any ties."

"Then why in God's name do I die a little every time I walk away from you?" he asked curtly. "Why do I wake up with your name on my lips?"

"I can't be your lover!" she whispered. "I can't!"

His nose brushed against hers, his lips hovered above her mouth, teasing it, coaxing it to follow his. "It would be so easy," he said softly, in a voice like dark velvet. "So easy. All it would take is ten minutes alone together with my mouth on yours and my hands under your blouse, and you'd give yourself with glorious abandon, the way you wanted to before I went to rescue Martina. Remember?" he breathed against her lips. "Remember, Gabby? You stood in my arms and let me touch you, and we rocked together and moaned..."

"Jacob." She hid her hot face against him. "Jacob, don't, please!"

His hands slid slowly down her back until they reached her hips and brought them into the curve of his, holding her there, pressing her there, so that she knew all too well what he wanted of her.

"This is a public place," she managed to say weakly, clinging to him.

"Where you're safe," he replied thickly. "Because if I did this anywhere else, I couldn't help what would happen. I want you so much."

"This is only making it worse," she told him. She leaned her forehead against his chest. She could smell the tangy soap he used, the clean scent of the shirt he wore. Her hands spread over his hard muscles.

His breath quickened at the almost imperceptible movement. "Unbutton it." He breathed roughly. "Touch me there."

"There are people ... !"

"Yes." His lips touched her closed eyelids, her forehead. "Touch me."

She could hardly breathe at all. He was drowning her in sensation, and she loved him so much it was torture. It was just going to be harder to leave him, but how could she fight this? Part of her was frightened of his strength, but a larger part remembered how it had felt when he was tender, when he'd been so careful not to hurt her.

"I won't ever hurt you again," he whispered, lifting her fingers to the top button. "Not ever. I won't overpower you, or make crude remarks to you. I'll teach you to trust me, if it takes the rest of my life. Gabby..."

She closed her eyes. Tentatively her fingers fumbled the first button free. He tensed as she found the second, and the third. She stopped there, resting against him, and eased her fingers just inside. They tingled as they came in contact with firm muscle and curling hair.

He caught his breath, shifting his chest so that her fingers slid farther under the fabric.

"You did that," he reminded her in a sensuous undertone, "when I started to touch you under your nightgown, at the *finca*. Remember? You shifted and moved so that I could touch you more easily."

What she remembered most was the way it had felt when he'd touched her. Her eyes slowly opened, and he turned her face so that he could look into them.

His own eyes were black with desire; his face was hard and drawn, his lips were parted. "Yes, I like that," he whispered as she curled her nails against him and dragged them softly over his skin. "I like that." His chest rose and fell heavily and still his eyes held hers. "If we made love, you could do that to every inch of me. And I could do it to you, with my mouth."

She trembled. He felt it and drew her slowly into his arms. He stood like that, just holding her, in a strangely passionless embrace while the world became calm.

"Words," he said over her head, his tone light and solemn at the same time. "So potent... Until you came along, I'd never made love to a woman with my mind."

She stared out at the sailboats on the lake and involuntarily one hand pressed closer against him. "We're at an impasse," she said after a minute.

His cheek nudged her dark hair. "How?"

She laughed bitterly. "J.D., I'm leaving next Friday."

"Maybe," he said, and his arms tightened.

"Definitely." She pulled away from him, and he let her go immediately. She looked up. "Nothing has changed."

He let his eyes roam over her soft body. "At least you've stopped cringing."

"Thank you," she replied. "For removing the scars. Now I can go on to a lasting relationship."

"Why not have it with me?" he asked. "I'm well-off. I'm sexy—"

"You're unreliable," she said, interrupting him. "I want someone who doesn't know an Uzi from a blender!"

He sighed heavily, and his dark eyes were thoughtful. "I need a little time."

"Time won't help," she said. "You're hooked again. It's like the cigarettes, only worse. I can't live my life standing at windows and waiting for telephones to ring."

"You'll do that regardless."

She stopped dead and turned around, gaping at him. "What?"

"You'll do that anyway," he said matter-of-factly, watching her. He pulled a cigarette from his pocket with a what-the-hell smile and lit it. "You'll miss me. You'll want me. You're leaving the office, but the memories are portable and indestructible. You won't forget me any more than I'll forget you. We started something we haven't finished, and it's going to be between us all our lives."

"It's just sex!" she yelled at him.

Two young men walked past, grinned at J.D., and winked at Gabby, who was wishing she could sink into the sand. She hadn't even heard them approach.

She turned and fled back down the beach at a trot. J.D. was right beside her, effortlessly matching her steps and still smoking his cigarette. He finished it just as they reached the car, and he crushed it out before he joined her in the luxurious interior.

"It isn't just sex," he said, turning to face her, one arm across the back of the seat and an odd expression on his face. He smiled slowly. "But sex is going to be one big part of our relationship in the not-too-distant future."

She glared at him. "You'd be lucky!"

"No, you would," he said, cocking an eyebrow. "When I mind my manners, I'm a force to be reckoned with. What I did to you in that bed was all bad temper and irritation. What I did to you the morning before was what it's really like."

She couldn't control her heated response to that intimate remark. Her breasts tingled at the memory. His eyes dropped slowly to her breasts, and he smiled wickedly. Following his gaze, she saw why and crossed her arms over her chest.

"Too late," he murmured. "Your body will give you away every time. You haven't forgotten what we did together."

Her nostrils flared. "There are other men in the world."

"Sure," he agreed pleasantly. "But you don't want other men. You want me."

"Conceited ass," she enunciated clearly.

His fingers touched her mouth and parted her lips, as if their texture fascinated him.

"You risked your life for me," he said absently. "Why?"

She laughed nervously. "Maybe I just wanted to try out the gun."

He tilted her face up and leaned over to brush his mouth tenderly across her trembling lips. "Maybe there was a reason you don't want me to know," he murmured. He drew back and looked at her. "Hungry?"

The change of topic threw her. He had switched from lover to friendly companion in seconds. She managed a smile. "Yes. What did you have in mind?"

"Cheeseburgers, of course." He chuckled and started the car.

"I like those myself."

He glanced at her. "Let's talk," he said unexpectedly. "Really talk. I want to know everything about you. What you like to read, how it was to grow up in Texas, why you've never gotten involved with a man... everything."

That sounded intriguing. It suddenly occurred to her that she knew very little about him. What he liked and disliked, what he felt. She tried to read his face.

"Curious about me too?" he asked, glancing sideways. "I'll tell you anything you want to know."

She laughed uneasily. "'Anything' covers a lot of territory."

"And requires a hell of a lot of trust on my part," he added with a smile. "Anything, Gabby."

Total honesty. She stared down at her hands and wondered why they were trembling. She wasn't sure of his motives, of where this was leading. She looked up and all her uncertainty was on her face.

He reached over and caught one of her hands, lifting it to his thigh. Her palm tingled at the contact.

"Make me stay here," he said unexpectedly.

"What?" she asked.

"Make me stay," he repeated. His eyes caught hers briefly. "You can give me something that all the unholy little wars on earth couldn't. If you want me, show me. Give me a reason, half a reason, to settle down. And I might surprise you."

She stared out through the windshield and felt as if she were floating. It was a beginning that she wasn't sure she wanted. She might hold his interest briefly, until he tired of her body. But what then? He was offering nothing more than a liaison. He wasn't talking about permanent things like a house and children. Her eyes darkened with pain. Perhaps it would have been better if he hadn't gotten rid of her fear of him.

Her troubled eyes sought his profile, but it was as unreadable as ever. The only thing that gave her hope was the visible throbbing of his pulse and the searing desire in his eyes. He wanted her so desperately that she couldn't help wondering whether he didn't feel something for her, too. But it would take time to find out, and she wasn't going to withdraw her resignation. As much as it might hurt, in the long run it would be saner to leave him than to try to hold him. Gabby wasn't built for an affair. And she wasn't going to let him drag her into one, just to occupy himself while he decided between practicing law and soldiering.

Chapter Ten

They sat in a booth at a nearby fast-food restaurant, where J.D. put away three cheeseburgers, a large order of french fries, and two cups of coffee before Gabby's fascinated eyes.

"I'm a big man," he reminded her as he was finishing the third one.

"Yes, you are," she agreed with a smile, running her eyes over the spread of muscle under his chambray shirt.

His eyes narrowed with amusement. "Remembering what's under it?" he said softly, teasing her.

She flushed and grabbed her coffee cup, holding it like a weapon. "I thought this was a truce," she muttered.

"It is. But I fight dirty, remember?"

She looked, studying his hard face. "What was it like, those four years when you were a mercenary?" she asked.

He finished the cheeseburger and sipped his coffee, leaning back with a heavy sigh. "It was hard," he said. "Exciting. Rewarding, in more ways than just financial." He shrugged. "I suppose I was caught up in the romance of it at first, until I saw what I was getting into. One of the men I joined with was captured and thrown into jail the minute we landed in one emerging African country. He hadn't fired a shot, but he was executed just like the men who had."

She caught her breath. "But why?" she asked. "He was just..."

"We were interfering with the regime," he told her. "Despite all our noble reasons, we were breaking whatever law existed at that time. Shirt and I managed to get away. I owe him my life for his quick thinking. I was pretty new to the profession back then. I learned."

"He told me his name was Matthew," she remarked with a smile.

He cocked an eyebrow. "Be flattered. It was three years before I found that out."

She toyed with her crumpled napkin. "I liked him. I liked all of them."

"Shirt's quite a guy. He was the one who pushed me into law," he said with a laugh. "He thought I needed a better future than rushing around the world with a weapon."

"You think a lot of him," she observed.

He shrugged. "I never knew my father," he said after a minute. "Shirt looked out for me when we served in Vietnam together. I don't know—maybe he needed somebody too. His wife had died of cancer, and he didn't have anybody else except a brother in Milwaukee who still doesn't speak to him. I had Martina. I suppose Shirt became my father, in a sense."

She cupped her hands around her coffee mug and wondered what he'd say if she told him that Shirt had said the door to the past was closed for J.D. Probably he'd laugh it off, but she decided she didn't want to find out.

He looked up. "How about your family? Any sisters, brothers?"

She laughed softly. "No. I was an only child. My father owned a ranch, and my mother and grandfather and grandmother had gone to San Antonio on vacation. Mother met Dad then and ran away to marry him over the weekend." She grinned. "My grandparents were furious."

"I can imagine." He searched her face. "You look like your mother. How about him? Was he big?"

She shook her head. "My father was small and wiry and tough. He had to be, you see, to put up with Mama. She'd have killed a lesser man, but Dad didn't take orders. There were some great fights during my childhood."

He cocked an eyebrow. "Did they make up eventually?"

She sighed. "He'd send her roses, or bring her pretty things from town. And she'd kiss him and they'd go off alone and I'd go see Miss Patty who lived in a line cabin on the ranch.'' She grinned. ''I visited Miss Patty a lot.''

He chuckled. ''They say the making up can be pretty sweet.''

She studied his hard face. ''Yes, so I hear.''

He lifted his eyes to hers. ''We've had a royal falling out. Want to make up?''

She hesitated, and he concentrated on finishing his coffee and reaching for a cigarette.

''Sorry,'' he said quietly. ''I'm rushing things.''

Hesitantly, she reached across the table and touched the back of the big hand resting there. It jerked. Then it turned and captured hers in its rough warmth.

''J.D., what do you want from me?'' she asked.

''What do you think I want, Gabby?'' he asked in turn.

She gathered all her courage and put her worst fears into words. ''I think you want to make amends for what happened in Guatemala, before you fly off into the sun. I think you want to have an affair with me.''

"That's honest, at least," he said. His eyes fell to their clasped hands, and he watched his thumb rub softly against her slender fingers. "You want something more permanent, I gather."

She couldn't answer that without giving herself away. She drew her hand away from his with a light laugh. "Aren't we getting serious though?" she asked. "I need to go home, J.D. I left the laundry in the washing machine, and I've got a week's cleaning to do."

His face hardened. "Can't it wait until tomorrow?"

"Tomorrow's Sunday."

"So?"

She lifted her eyes to his. "I go to church on Sunday."

He frowned slightly. "I haven't been to church since I was a boy," he said after a minute. He studied the smoking cigarette in his hand. "I don't know what I believe in these days."

It was a reminder of the big differences between them. She frowned too, and got to her feet slowly.

"It would bother you," he murmured, watching her. "Yes, I suppose it would."

She half turned. "What would?"

"Never mind." He sighed as he put the remains of their meal into the trash can and replaced the tray in the rack on their way out. "Just a few adjustments that have to be made, that's all."

That didn't make sense, but she didn't pressure him. He didn't pressure her either, leaving her outside her apartment building with a rueful smile.

"I hate being stood up for the damned laundry," he muttered, hands in his pockets.

"New experiences teach new things," she murmured dryly. "Besides, I can't finish out the week in dirty clothes."

That put a damper on things. Her smile faded at the memory of how little time they had left together. His face grew harder.

"Well...thanks for lunch," she said awkwardly.

"We could do it again tomorrow," he said before she went inside.

Her eyes lifted. She wanted to. She wanted to, desperately. She tried to convince herself that it would be a mistake, but her body tingled and her heart surged at the idea.

"Yes," she said under her breath.

His chest rose and fell, as if in relief. "Suppose I pick you up about ten-thirty?"

She hesitated. "Church is at eleven."

"Yes, I figured it would be," he said with a rueful smile. "I hope the angels won't faint at having me in their midst."

All the color drained out of her face as she stared up at him, and she couldn't have said a word to save herself.

"Well, I won't embarrass you," he muttered curtly. "I do know not to stand up and yell 'Hallelujah' every five minutes or to snore in the front pew."

"I didn't say anything," she said.

"I still have a soul too, even if it has taken a few hard knocks over the years." He lifted his shoulders and let them fall. "I...need to go back. All the way back." His eyes held hers. "Gabby?"

"I'm Methodist," she said.

He smiled. "I used to be Episcopalian. The denomination doesn't matter so much, does it?"

She shook her head. "We can walk from my apartment."

He nodded. "See you tomorrow."

He turned to get back into the car, but she moved forward and touched his arm. The light contact of her fingers froze him. He looked down at her.

"Would you...bend down a minute?" she whispered.

Like a sleepwalker, he bent his tall frame and she stood on tiptoe to put her mouth warmly, hungrily to his.

He moaned, starting to reach for her, but she drew back with a wicked, warm smile.

"Try that again when we aren't in a public place," he said, challenging her.

Her heart jumped. "Dream on."

He lifted an eyebrow. "I've done very little else this past week," he said, letting his eyes roam over her slender body. "Gabby, have you ever thought about having children?"

She could hardly believe what she was hearing. Her face burned with pleasure, her heart sang with it. "Oh, yes," she whispered huskily.

"So have I." He started to speak, caught himself, and smiled hesitantly. "See you in the morning."

"'Bye." She stood there and watched him drive off. It was probably all some wild daydream and she'd wake up back in the office, typing. But when she pinched herself, it hurt. She went upstairs and put the clothes in the dryer and tried to convince herself that J.D. had actually said he was going to church with her.

But the next morning, she was sure she'd misunderstood him. She dressed in a pretty Gibson Girl-style white outfit with matching accessories and at precisely ten-thirty, she started out the door. Of course, J.D. wasn't going to church, she told herself firmly. What a stupid thing to...

The doorbell rang as she was opening the door. And there he was. He was wearing the same vested gray suit she'd seen him in earlier that week, but he looked different now. More relaxed, more at ease, much less rigid.

"Shocked?" he asked wickedly. "Did you expect I'd changed my mind and gone fishing instead?"

She burst out laughing and her green eyes sparkled. With her long hair piled in an old-fashioned coiffure, she seemed part of another era.

"Little Miss Victorian," he murmured, studying her. "How exciting you look. So demure and proper."

He looked as if he'd give a lot to change that straight-laced image, and she dropped her eyes before he could see how willing she felt.

"We'd better get started," she murmured, easing past him.

"I like that gauzy thing," he remarked minutes later as they walked up the front steps of the gray fieldstone church.

"You can wear it sometimes, if you like," she said teasingly.

His eyes promised retribution. She eased her hand into his, and all the fight went out of him. He smiled at her, and his eyes were warm and possessive.

J.D. paid a lot of attention to the sermon, which was about priorities and forgiveness and grace. He sang the hymns in a rich baritone, and he seemed thoughtful as the benediction was given.

"Mind waiting for me?" he asked as they rose to file out at the end of the service.

She searched his hard face and shook her head. "Not at all."

He left her and went to speak to the minister who was waiting until the rest of the congregation had left. The two men stood talking behind the rows of pews, both solemn, their voices low. Then they shook hands and smiled at each other. J.D. came back and grasped Gabby's hand warmly in his for a minute.

"I'm taking your minister to lunch instead of you," he said with a mischievous smile. "How about getting into something casual and I'll pick you up in a couple of hours?"

She looked hard at him. "Are you all right?" she asked. She was trying to see beyond the fixed smile to something deep and wounded inside him.

He drew in a slow breath and the smile faded. "You frighten me sometimes, Gabby," he said softly. "You see too much."

She couldn't think of any response to that. She touched his hand briefly and watched him walk away. Something was in the wind, a change. She frowned as she turned toward her apartment, her steps slow and deliberate. She wondered why he was taking her minister to lunch, if he had something on his conscience.

She changed into jeans and a button-up blue cotton blouse and then paced the floor for the next two hours. Wild thoughts raced through her mind, the wildest one being that J.D. might decide to chuck it all and go in search of First Shirt and Apollo.

It was three hours before he showed up. By then Gabby had consumed half a pot of coffee and chewed two fingernails to the quick. Her nerves were raw, and she actually jumped when the knock came at the door.

She let him in, too shaken to disguise the frightened uncertainty in her wide eyes.

"I thought you'd stood me up." She laughed nervously. "I was just about to give up and start watching a movie on TV. Do you want some coffee, or some cake . . . ?"

He put a finger across her mouth to stop the wild words. His dark eyes looked into hers. "We have to learn to trust each other a little more," he said softly. "And the first thing you need to know about me is that if I ever give my word, it's good for life. I'm not going back to Shirt and the others, Gabby. That's a promise."

Tears burst from her eyes like rain from a storm cloud. She put her face in her hands and walked away.

"I'm sorry," she choked out, hating the fact that she'd given her feelings away.

He didn't say a word. He followed her, and when he caught up to her, he lifted her gently in his big arms and headed straight for the bedroom.

She had just enough sanity left to realize where they were going. She opened her mouth to protest, and his came down on it, open and moist and tenderly possessive.

"Jacob..." she whispered into his mouth.

He smiled against her trembling lips. "What?"

Her nails bit softly into his shoulders as he laid her down on the crisp white chenille bedspread. "I can't," she whispered.

"Can't what?" He sat down beside her and calmly removed his jacket, vest, and tie and then unbuttoned his shirt while she watched him, spellbound as the hard, heavy muscles came into view under that mat of crisp hair.

"I can't have an affair with you," she said.

He leaned over and began to unfasten the buttons on her blouse. "That's nice."

"Jacob, did you hear me? Will you stop that...!"

He ignored her protests and her frantic efforts to stop his fingers. "Stop what?"

"Undressing me!" she burst out with an hysterical laugh. "Jacob, I'm wearing nothing underneath, for heaven's sake...!"

"So I see," he murmured with a wicked smile, as he opened the blouse and revealed the pink and mauve rise of her breasts.

"Will you listen..." she began breathlessly.

"Shut up, darling." He bent over her and put his open mouth against one breast, letting her feel the texture of his warm lips and his tongue before he moved closer and increased the ardent pressure.

She gasped and arched and then moaned sharply, a high-pitched sound that made him lift his head.

"Did I hurt you?" he asked. "I'm sorry, I thought I was being gentle."

Her fists were clenched beside her head, and her eyes were wide with mingled fear and desire. "You know very well it didn't hurt," she whispered fiercely.

His eyes moved back down to her bareness and he smiled slowly, watching her breasts lift and fall with her quickened breathing. "Lovely, lovely creature," he said under his breath. His fingers traced her rib cage and he held her eyes, watching the recklessness come into them, the deep passion.

Her breath was coming still quicker now, and the tracing of his fingers was driving her mad. She arched her head back into the pillow, lifting her body toward him in a slow, helpless movement.

"Want me to put my mouth there again and make it stop aching?" he whispered.

"Yes," she moaned softly. "Please."

She felt the whisper of his warm breath against her skin, felt his hands go under her to slide abrasively against her bare back. He lifted her, and his mouth moved with delicate precision from one taut breast to the other. His face nuzzled her, savored her softness.

Her fingers tangled in his thick, cool hair and worked at it like a cat kneading a blanket. Pleasure washed over her in waves, waves that lifted and twisted her body.

"Jacob," she whispered as his mouth slid over hers and down to her ear, while his hands made magic on her upthrust breasts. "Jacob, teach me how to make you feel this way."

"I already do," he murmured at her ear. "Touching you like this, kissing you, makes me wild, didn't you know?"

"Really?"

He lifted his head. "Really." He rolled onto his back and eased her down over him, smiling lazily as he studied her rapt face, as his eyes wandered to where her breasts were crushed softly against his hard, hair-matted chest. His hands unfastened her hair and arranged it over her shoulders, his eyes heavy-lidded and steady as they wandered over her body.

She watched his face and moved. Just a little. Just enough to let him feel the texture of her body.

"Is that an invitation?" he asked quietly, watching her.

Her breath caught in her throat. Was it, indeed? She searched his hard face with awe and love in every line of her own. Her fingers twined in his thick hair, and she could feel his heartbeat under her.

His hands smoothed over her back. He shifted her body this time, softly rubbing her breasts against the mat of hair on his chest.

He heard her catch her breath as she bent her forehead to rest it on his.

His hands shifted, so that his thumbs could tease the hard peaks of her breasts. "I ache with wanting you," he said quietly. "Shall I let you feel how much?"

"You started it," she reminded him, nuzzling her forehead against his. She moved suddenly, so that the whole soft length of her body pressed down over him, and she knew then that she wasn't going to stop him.

"Hold me like this," she whispered as she bent to put her mouth over his. "Hold me hard, Jacob."

His big hands spread at the base of her spine, moving her in a sweet, tender rotation against his hips, and he moaned deeply.

"I won't stop you this time," she whispered over his mouth. "I won't stop you, Jacob, I won't..." Her hands slid between them, into the thick cloud of hair over his chest. "Jacob...!"

"Tell me...why," he managed to say in a tortured voice.

"You know," she breathed, crushing her mouth against his in a frenzy of hunger. Her body moved against him, she trembled with unleashed desire. And suddenly he rolled her over, covering her with his crushing weight, lifting her up to him while his mouth possessed hers absolutely. She felt the wild, demanding thrust of his tongue and met it with a wildness of her own, giving him everything he demanded of her.

"Tell me," he insisted, lifting his head to let his wild eyes glitter down into her own. He shifted, grinding his hips into hers. "Tell me, Gabby!"

"I love you," she said fiercely. Her voice was trembling, but she met his eyes unafraid. "I love you, I love you!"

He seemed to stop breathing. His body was rigid above her, but his eyes were alive, burning, blazing with emotion. His hands moved slowly up her body, over her breasts, to touch her face. His big body shuddered with the effort to control his passion.

"I'm going to die from this," he told her with a faint, harsh smile. And all at once, he rolled away from her and lay on his stomach. He groaned once, as if he were hurting in unbearable ways. His body stiffened and he clenched the pillow so hard his fingers went white.

"Jacob?" she whispered, sitting up, frightened.

"Don't touch me, baby," he whispered back, his voice tormented.

She sat there watching him, a little nervous and uncertain. He'd forced that reckless admission from her, and then he'd stopped. Why? What did he want?

Slowly his body relaxed and he sighed wearily. "Oh, God, I never thought I'd be able to stop," he murmured. "That was as close as I've ever come to losing control, except for that time at the *finca*."

Her wide eyes studied the pale face he turned toward her. "That morning?" she murmured.

He laughed dryly. "That night," he said. "Gabby, it wasn't punishment, there at the last. It was loss of control. I very nearly took you."

Her eyebrows went up. "But you let me think...!"

"I had to," he said. "I was going out of my mind trying to decide how to handle it.

In the beginning, I wanted an affair with you. But I couldn't seem to get close enough, or make you see me as a man. Then, when we were in Rome, I'd had all I could stand and I forced the issue." He laughed softly. "My God, it was the end of the rainbow, and I was floating. Until I realized you were a virgin, and I had to rethink it all. I'd decided that I'd have to fire you, and then we went into the jungle and I died a thousand deaths when that terrorist pointed his rifle at you." He rolled over onto his back and caught her fingers in his, holding them to his mouth feverishly. "That was when I realized what had happened to me. I was like a boy, all raging desire and frustration and fear. I wanted to frighten you off before I was trapped by what I felt for you. Only it backfired. I started to hurt you and went crazy wanting you instead. I can't wait anymore," he added with an apologetic smile, "and after a week from Saturday I won't have to."

"A week from Saturday?" She frowned.

"There were two reasons I took your Reverend Boone to lunch," he said. "The first was to discuss some things I had on my conscience. The second was to arrange a wedding.''

She froze; her face was flushed, and her eyes were disbelieving. It was like having every dream she had ever dreamed come true at once.

He sat up, taking both her hands in his. ''Gabby, the one thing I can't do is go on living without you,'' he said matter-of-factly.

''But...but you said you didn't know whether you could settle down.''

He rubbed his thumbs over the backs of her hands and sighed. ''Yes, I know. And all the while I was wondering how I'd survive if you refused me. I was trying to get a reaction out of you, to see if I'd frightened you so badly that I'd chased you away.'' His face hardened as he stared at her hands. ''I told you once that I was used to taking what I wanted. That ended with you. I couldn't take you. It had to be a mutual wanting.''

''It was,'' she breathed softly. ''It is. I love you with all my heart.''

He smiled quietly, lifting hungry eyes to hers. "Do you know what I feel for you?"

She lifted her shoulders restlessly. "You want me," she said with a shaky smile. "Maybe you like me a little."

His chest rose and fell heavily and his eyes never left hers. "I've never said the words and meant them before. It's harder than I thought."

She moved close to him and slid her arms under his, pressing her cheek against his broad chest.

His hands hesitated on her back and then slid around her, cherishing, comforting, protective. He sighed, and she felt his breath on her ear.

"I..." He nuzzled his face against her cheek and then her throat. He laid her back on the bed so that he could find her soft breasts and brush them with his lips. His teeth nipped her tenderly, his hands lifted her. With a sound like a rough, low growl, he slid his body alongside hers and kissed her until she moaned and clutched at him.

"I love you," he breathed fiercely, looming over her. His face was so taut with passion that it would have frightened her once. "Worship you, adore you. I'll go down into the dark crying your name, wanting your mouth, your voice. Is that enough?"

Tears welled in her eyes. "Oh, yes, it's enough," she said unsteadily. "But will I be enough for you?"

"Yes," he said simply. "You and the children." He bent to her mouth again. "Reverend Boone said you hadn't joined the church. I thought we'd do it together. The kids are going to need a good foundation to build on, aren't they?"

She hid her face against his throat. "I'll like having your babies," she whispered.

He trembled convulsively. "Say things like that to me, and you'll find yourself wearing scarlet at the wedding. Hush!"

She managed to laugh. "You taught me how."

"That isn't all I'll teach you. But not now." He rolled away from her and got to his feet reluctantly, stretching as if his muscles were in torment.

She propped herself on an elbow and smiled at him wistfully. "You've got to be the sexiest man alive," she murmured. "I used to stare at you in the office and wonder what you looked like without your shirt . . ."

"Gabby," he said in a mock threatening tone.

She arched her body softly, wanting him, loving him, loving the way his eyes followed her movement with such obvious hunger.

"Jacob," she whispered, lying back so that the blouse slid away from her body and he could see every soft curve.

His chest rose and fell sharply. He seemed a little unsteady on his feet.

She loved that vulnerability. She'd never realized before just how much power she had over him, and it was a heady knowledge. With a small, triumphant smile, she held out her arms to him.

"I can't, honey," he whispered. "If I come back down there, I'll take you."

Her body tingled with the very thought of how it would be. She could already picture them, his hair-darkened body crushing her bare pink one down into the mattress, his voice whispering those wildly exciting things while she moaned and wept . . .

He reached down, and she arched toward him. And all at once, before she realized what was going on, she was out of the bed, being buttoned back into her blouse.

"And don't try that again," he murmured with a wicked smile. "Hussy."

"But..."

"When we're married," he said firmly, kissing her mouth. "Now let's go look at houses. I drove by two yesterday that looked promising. How do you feel about living on the lake?"

She slid her hand into his as they walked into the living room. "I'll like living anywhere with you," she said with feeling. "I imagine just watching television is going to be an adventure from now on."

He chuckled softly as he opened the door, his eyes narrowing. "You can't imagine the plans I have for the symphony concerts on the educational channel," he remarked with a wicked smile.

She went ahead of him out the door. "Oh, I think I might have some vague idea," she said musingly, glancing over her shoulder.

"By the way, what did you do with the crossbow?"

"What crossbow?" he asked grinning.

She sighed and leaned her head against his shoulder for an instant. "Do you reckon First Shirt would give me away if we asked him?"

"I imagine he'd be pretty flattered," he said. "Want to invite the rest of the gang too?"

"Could we?"

"Sure," he told her. He smiled as they got into the elevator. "Don't look so worried. I won't try to leave with them, I promise."

"No regrets?" she asked softly.

His eyes were wistful for a moment before he sighed and drew her into his arms. "Only," he whispered, bending, "that I waited so long to tell you how I felt."

"So long?"

"Gabby," he said against her mouth, "I fell in love with you two years ago."

She started to speak, but he was kissing her, and the wildness of it made her question go right out of her head.

"You never said anything," she murmured eventually.

"I couldn't," he returned. "You were so young. I felt guilty for wanting you the way I did. But you dated, you seemed so sophisticated sometimes." He touched her hair gently. "I had too many doubts about being able to settle down to make a heavy pass at you. Too, I was afraid you might quit, and I wasn't sure I could stand that." He shrugged his broad shoulders. "It wasn't until that day in the jungle that I knew how much I cared. I spent a miserable weekend trying to convince myself that I could go back to what I was and not miss you. I failed. After that, it was a matter of trying to convince you that I wouldn't be brutal again. You can't imagine how it hurt, when you cringed away from me..."

But she could. The anguish was in his face. She reached up and kissed his closed eyes gently, tenderly. "It wasn't so much a physical fear," she confessed, "as an emotional one. I was afraid you only wanted an affair. And that you'd walk away." She laughed bitterly. "I knew I couldn't survive that. I loved you too much."

"We won't be apart again," he said quietly. "Not ever. Even when you have the children, I'll be with you every step of the way."

Tears misted her eyes. "I'll like that."

Six days later, there was a quiet ceremony in the Methodist church. Gabby, in a street-length white silk dress, walked slowly down the aisle on the arm of a wiry little man in a new gray suit, who looked even more out of place than the other people in the church. A tall black man standing beside J.D. was tugging uncomfortably at his tight collar and tie, and several other awkward-looking men were sitting in the front pew. Gabby noticed Richard Dice and two secretaries who worked in her building casting strange glances at the assembly. Her mother seemed equally perplexed.

Gabby just grinned and walked on, feeling proud and happy as J.D. grinned at her from where he stood near the altar.

It was a brief but solemn ceremony, and at its end, after Gabby had enthusiastically kissed her new husband, she threw her arms around Matthew and hugged him.

"Thank you," she told him with a beaming smile.

First Shirt looked faintly embarrassed. "I enjoyed it. Uh, Gabby, your mother's giving us a strange look."

"Mother's always been strange, Matthew," she informed him. "I'll show you. Mother, come meet Matthew," she called while J.D.'s partner Richard congratulated him and bent to kiss Gabby's cheek.

"All the best, Gabby, J.D.," Richard said with a grin. "What a shock, to be invited to your wedding. Especially after all that's happened the past week."

"The road to love is rocky," Gabby grinned at him. "As you'll discover someday."

"Not me," Richard retorted. "I run too fast!"

"That's what I thought," J.D. murmured with a wicked glance toward Gabby. She stuck out her tongue at him, and went to drag her mother away from the secretaries.

Mrs. Darwin, resplendent in a white linen suit and a hat that looked three sizes too big, followed her daughter slowly. She looked as out of place as Matthew and Apollo and the rest.

"I hate dressing up," she muttered, casting a curious eye at Matthew. "Give me my jeans anytime."

"I hear you shoot and cuss and ride," Matthew told her, pursing his lips.

Mrs. Darwin actually blushed. She lowered her eyes and grinned. "Well, a little, Mr...?"

"Matthew," came the reply. "Matthew Carver. Archer's...I mean, J.D.'s like a son to me." He held out his hand, took hers, and lifted it to his lips. "What a lovely mother-in-law he's getting," he murmured.

Gabby left her blushing mother and went to greet Apollo, Semson, Laremos, and Drago.

"Hi, guys," she said, grinning at them.

"Hey, Gabby," Apollo greeted her. "Good thing you know the ropes—we won't have to run you through the training course or anything."

"Now, just hold on," she informed him. "I am going on a honeymoon. My adventuring days are over. I can just see me, pregnant and crawling through underbrush with an AK-47..."

"Oh, we'd carry it for you, Gabby," he said, all seriousness.

"How gentlemanly!" She laughed.

"Unspeakable ruffian," Laremos said with a mock frown as he stepped forward to kiss Gabby's hand. "Congratulations. And of course you will not be crawling through the jungle." He grinned. "We will carry you."

Semson and Drago added their comments, and Gabby clutched J.D.'s arm, all but collapsing with laughter.

A strange man stood up farther down the pew and walked closer as the other guests paused on their way out to congratulate Gabby and J.D. He was the last. Tall, blond, and heavily muscled, he had a face as rugged as Jacob's and a tan that emphasized his sun-bleached hair.

He had brown eyes, and they studied Gabby for a long moment before he spoke.

He was wearing a tan suit that looked as new as those J.D.'s men friends had on, and there was something familiar about the way he shook hands with J.D.

"I thought you hated weddings," J.D. remarked with a cool smile.

"I do. I just wanted to see who caught you." He pursed his lips and narrowed one eye, looking Gabby over in a way that made her nervous. Finally, one corner of his mouth tugged up a little and he gave a short laugh. "Well, if she can shoot and doesn't start screaming at gunfire, I guess she's okay."

"Okay?" she returned with a cold stare. "I'll have you know I'm terrific. I can even hit what I aim at."

The laugh mellowed a little and his dark eyes twinkled. "Can you?" He held out his hand. "I'm Dutch."

Her eyes widened. She remembered that he'd met J.D. in Rome and was the intelligence-gathering logistics man for the team.

"Well, miracles never cease," she murmured. "I thought you'd be bowlegged and chew tobacco."

Dutch burst out laughing. Impulsively, he drew her into a friendly embrace and hugged her. "Oh, J.D., you lucky son of a..."

"Dutch!" First Shirt burst out, interrupting him. "Where did you come from?"

"Lebanon," came the reply. "I need a few grunts. Interested?"

"Maybe," Matthew said. He glanced at the others. "Let's go talk. J.D., take care of her. And yourself." He clasped hands with the younger man. "I'll be in touch."

Gabby hugged him. "Thanks for giving me away. Let me know where you'll be at Christmas. I'll send you a box of thick socks."

Matthew kissed her forehead. "I'll do that." He leaned toward her ear. "Write down your mama's address for me too," he added in a whisper. "I like a lady who can shoot and cuss."

She laughed. "I'll do that."

The others filed out after brief goodbyes, and Gabby glanced at J.D.'s impassive face as they thanked Reverend Boone and started on their way to take Gabby's mother back to the airport.

"Call me once in a while, baby," her mother said to Gabby at the entrance to the waiting area.

"I will." She hugged the older woman. "Matthew took to you."

Her mother grinned. "I took to him too."

"There's just one thing..." Gabby began, wondering how much to tell her mother.

"He'll settle one day, just like J.D. did," came the quiet reply, and her mother gave her a knowing smile. "Some men take longer. Meanwhile, I write a sweet letter." She winked. "Come and visit."

"We will," J.D. promised, coming up to join them. He hugged his new mother-in-law and watched as she walked away with a wave.

Gabby slid her hand into the crook of his arm, and they walked back toward the parking lot.

"You've been very quiet since we left the church," he said softly. "Were you afraid I'd want to go with them?"

She was startled by his perception. "Yes, I think so. A little," she admitted.

He stopped beside the car and turned her to him, looking down into her troubled face. "I'll be honest with you, because anything less would cheat us both. I did feel a sense of loss when the others left without me, because in Guatemala I had a taste of the old, wild life and it brought back memories of days when I had more freedom than I have now. But I'm a realist, Gabby. Matthew said he told you, before we left Guatemala, that I'd gone too far to come back to them, to their way of life." She nodded and he touched her mouth softly with his fingers. "He was right. I've built a future for myself, for you. I've invested too much of my life in building it to throw it away for a little excitement. Besides," he murmured, lifting her slender hand to his chest and pressing it hard, "there are different levels of excitement."

His eyes studied hers with an intensity that made her knees go weak. He slid her fingers inside his vest, against his white shirt, letting her feel the warmth of his skin and the thunder of his pulse.

"You have the same effect on me that being caught under fire does," he whispered huskily, moving her fingers across one hard male nipple. "Except that you're a little less dangerous than a bullet."

"Only a little?" she whispered back, moving close, so that she could feel the length of his body touching hers.

His dark head bent and his mouth hovered just above hers. His hand moved between them to stroke one soft, high breast. It immediately went taut; his nostrils flared and his eyes burned with undisguised hunger.

"Are you afraid to have sex with me?" he whispered.

Her face flushed, but she didn't drop her eyes. "No. I love you," she whispered. "And it won't be sex. It will be...loving."

His mouth parted hers softly, sensuously. "In broad daylight, Gabby," he breathed.

"Yes, I know," she murmured, meeting his lips hungrily. "We can watch each other."

He looked into her eyes and saw the wildest kind of jungle there. He bent and caught her against him, kissing her hungrily and hard, feeling her response. He could hardly catch his breath when he finally lifted his head. "I don't need to go looking for adventure anymore. Not while I have you," he said gruffly. "A woman with an adventurous heart is excitement enough for me."

"Take me home, Jacob," she whispered. "Teach me."

He looked into her misty eyes and reluctantly let her go. "What an utterly delicious thought." He laughed unsteadily, and the lessons were already in his eyes. She looked at him and saw them as they would be, mouth to mouth, his body over hers, hard and warm and ardent, her eyes looking into his as they came together on crisp, cool sheets with his dark body overwhelming her soft, pink one with the same pleasure she felt when he stroked her bare flesh, only much more intimate, more intense...

She trembled softly in anticipation, wanting to be alone with him, wanting his hands, his mouth, his absolute possession. "I can hardly wait," she said, her voice trembling.

He put her into the car and paused for an instant, glancing toward the sky where a military plane was passing over. His face hardened for an instant as he stood quietly watching it until it was out of sight. But when he climbed in beside Gabby and looked at her glowing face, her bright, loving eyes, the hardness drained away. His dark eyes narrowed with the first stirrings of possession. And he smiled.

*   *   *   *   *

If you just can't get enough of

Diana Palmer

you can find her at your favorite
retail outlet in June with

THE TENDER STRANGER

The Soldier of Fortune trilogy continues as
hard-edged mercenary Eric van Meer finds
he's in danger—of losing his heart—when
he meets Dani St. Clair. All that had come
before in his life was nothing compared to
the danger his heart now faced...

Look for the last title in this passionate
trilogy—ENAMORED—in August.

Only from  *Silhouette*®

_{TM}

where passion lives.

DP4

Take 3 of "The Best of the Best™" Novels FREE

Plus get a FREE surprise gift!

Special Limited-time Offer

Mail to The Best of the Best™

3010 Walden Avenue
P.O. Box 1867
Buffalo, N.Y. 14269-1867

YES! Please send me 3 free novels and my free surprise gift. Then send me 3 of "The Best of the Best™" novels each month. I'll receive the best books by the world's hottest romance authors. Bill me at the low price of $3.74 each plus 25¢ delivery and applicable sales tax, if any.* That's the complete price and—compared to the cover prices of $4.50 each—quite a bargain! I understand that accepting the books and gift places me under no obligation ever to buy any books. I can always return a shipment and cancel at any time. Even if I never buy another book from Harlequin, the 3 free books and the surprise gift are mine to keep forever.

183 BPA ANV9

Name	(PLEASE PRINT)	
Address	Apt. No.	
City	State	Zip

This offer is limited to one order per household and not valid to current subscribers.
*Terms and prices are subject to change without notice. Sales tax applicable in N.Y.
 All orders subject to approval.

UBOB-94

©1990 Harlequin Enterprises Limited

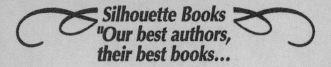

Silhouette Books
"Our best authors, their best books...

DIANA PALMER
Soldier of Fortune in February

ELIZABETH LOWELL
Dark Fire in February

LINDA LAEL MILLER
Ragged Rainbow in March

JOAN HOHL
California Copper in March

LINDA HOWARD
An Independent Wife in April

HEATHER GRAHAM POZZESSERE
Double Entendre in April

When it comes to passion, we wrote the book.

Silhouette®

SPRING
fancy
'94

They're sexy, single...
and about to get snagged!

Passion is in full bloom as love catches
the fancy of three brash bachelors. You won't
want to miss these stories by three of
Silhouette's hottest authors:

CAIT LONDON
DIXIE BROWNING
PEPPER ADAMS

Spring fever is in the air this March—
and there's no avoiding it!

Only from

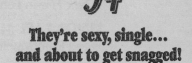

where passion lives.

SF94

It's our 1000th
Silhouette Romance
and we're celebrating!

Join us for a special collection of love stories by the authors you've
loved for years, and new favorites you've just discovered.

It's a celebration just for you,
with wonderful books by
Diana Palmer, Suzanne Carey,
Tracy Sinclair, Marie Ferrarella,
Debbie Macomber, Laurie Paige,
Annette Broadrick, Elizabeth August
and MORE!

Silhouette Romance...vibrant, fun and emotionally rich! Take another
look at us!

As part of the celebration, readers can receive a FREE gift AND enter
our exciting sweepstakes to win a grand prize of $1000! Look for
more details in all March Silhouette series titles.

You'll fall in love all over again
with Silhouette Romance!

Silhouette®

CEL1000T

Don't miss these additional titles by favorite author

DIANA PALMER!

Silhouette Desire®

#05715	THE CASE OF THE CONFIRMED BACHELOR+	$2.89	❏
#05733	THE CASE OF THE MISSING SECRETARY+	$2.89	❏
#05799	NIGHT OF LOVE*	$2.99	❏
#05829	SECRET AGENT MAN*	$2.99	❏

+ Most Wanted Series
*Man of the Month

Silhouette Romance™

#08910	EMMETT*	$2.69	❏

°Long, Tall Texans

#08971	KING'S RANSOM	$2.75	❏

Silhouette® Books

#48242	DIANA PALMER COLLECTION (2-in-1 collection)	$4.59	❏
#48254	TO MOTHER WITH LOVE '93	$4.99	❏

(short-story collection also featuring Debbie Macomber and Judith Duncan)

#48267	HEATHER'S SONG	$4.50	❏
#48268	FIRE AND ICE	$4.50	❏
#48269	THE AUSTRALIAN	$4.50	❏

TOTAL AMOUNT	$
POSTAGE & HANDLING	$
($1.00 for one book, 50¢ for each additional)	
APPLICABLE TAXES**	$ _____
TOTAL PAYABLE	$ _____
(check or money order—please do not send cash)	

To order, complete this form and send it, along with a check or money order for the total above, payable to Silhouette Books, to: **In the U.S.:** 3010 Walden Avenue, P.O. Box 9077, Buffalo, NY 14269-9077; **In Canada:** P.O. Box 636, Fort Erie, Ontario, L2A 5X3.

Name: _____

Address: _____ City: _____

State/Prov.: _____ Zip/Postal Code: _____

**New York residents remit applicable sales taxes.
Canadian residents remit applicable GST and provincial taxes.

DPBACK5

Silhouette ®